Lamberton -

LuAnn Vinden

REHEARSALS FOR ARMAGEDDON

by David C. Hon

Third Printing

Cover design:
Arthur Zapel

Publisher:
Arthur Meriwether Inc.
921 Curtiss St.
Downers Grove, IL.
60515

ISBN 0-916260-01-1

NON-PROFESSIONAL PERFORMANCES

To encourage amateur public production of these plays non-professional production rights will be granted for non-playing houses and non-profit endeavors provided that Contemporary Drama Service, Box 457, Downers Grove, Ill. is notified of all dates and locations and that at least one copy of this book is purchased for each performer. Minimum purchases for non-royalty performance are:

Glass Houses - 1 book
War Surplus - 6 books
Airplane - 8 books
Beat the Press - 6 books
Visiting Hours - 5 books
Gunfight - 6 books
The Mannequin - 4 books
The First Athiest Church - 1 book
Murder Mystery - 7 books

PROFESSIONAL AND SEMI-PROFESSIONAL PERFORMANCES

Several royalty arrangements are available for professional and semi-professional performers. Write: Business Manager, Contemporary Drama Service, Box 457, Downers Grove, Ill. 60515. Explain your intended use. Straight royalty or percentage of gross ticket sales performances are available options.

Manufactured in the United States of America

PREFACE

The theatrical urge hits one in strange places. Some it hits in the spine and others it hits in the gray matter. It has been known to infect whole populations in isolated cities of the hinterlands with no apparent cause. No walk of life seems immune from this urge, and no race, religion, or creed serves as effective serum.

It hit me in a town high in the Andes of Peru. I had been lecturing to English language institutes in several major cities in Peru, and had for several months prior to that been teaching upper level conversation classes. I had been commenting about how these students needed some simple short plays with compelling interest yet simple in context, and as dawn rose in the High Sierra one morning it occured to me that there were few playwrights embarked on such a task. And so I set about scribbling.

Cause and effect, however, are sometimes total strangers. So it was that I packed up, plays and all, and accepted a teaching position at Oklahoma College of Liberal Arts. Directoral classes needed short plays there, and the plays intended to teach English ended up helping to teach the theatrical idiom.

Then a group of enthusiatic students took up all that I had written and had a night of "underground" one-acts. When this generated enough interest to travel, the concept of the miniature repertory theatre was born. This concept follows, and the plays in this book, though usable separately, were designed to implement it.

David C. Hon

The Miniature Repertory Theatre

The concept of a miniature repertory company has often been used in commercial comedy to present a lively assortment of sketches in a fast-paced mosaic. Rarely, however, is that same motif employed for serious theatre.

Dealing with several short one-act plays of ten to fifteen minutes each, a group of eight people could fashion a unique evening of entertainment via this mini-repertory concept. If the repertory included twelve short one-act plays, the director could reshape his program nightly for the time allotted, for the physical set-up, and for the audience which would be watching. And in changing at least half the program each night the director could insure that those who return to his show would continually have new experiences.

The plays herein are written for the above-mentioned context. They are bare stage with a few simple props, scant costume requirements, minimal lighting, varying - but small - cast requirements and, hopefully, will be plays which touch contemporary nerve centres.

The advantages of such a concept for schools is obvious:-

(1) Maximum variety of roles for actors of the company.

(2) Maximum creativity for the director, who must not only make viable plays from the bare ground up, but who must mold his theatre nightly to time, space, and audience requirements.

(3) Minimal transportation, in that all properties, costumes and players can be put comfortably into two average-sized automobiles.

The plays herein represent an evening of entertainment. Although they could well be used for acting and directing classes on both high school and college levels (for each is a completely separate entity), their real value is as part of a living phenomenon, a miniature repertory theatre which is at once variable, vital, and available.

Contents

* Flexible cast requirements.

NOTE: These plays were first professional performed December, 1973 at the Dudley Riggs Theatre, Minneapolis, Minnesota and were directed by Michael Brindisi.

NOTE: The numerals running vertically down the left margin of each page of dialogue are for the convenience of the director. With these he may easily direct attention to a specific passage.

Glass Houses

a one-act play by

David C. Hon

Cast - One housewife

Setting - Completely blank stage

(Lights On. Housewife is in the middle of the stage, holding a rag and a bottle of Windex. Her hair is tied up with a scarf and she wears a man's shirt and women's jeans.)

Housewife: See this (Holds up Windex) Best glass cleaner I've ever used...

(Sprays and wipes an imaginary window between herself and audience.)

Housewife: See?...So clean you can't even tell there is glass there, can you?

(Knocks on imaginary glass. Knocking sound offstage accompanies.)

Housewife: (Holding Windex to breast) And when you live in an all-glass house like I do, this becomes pretty important, let me tell you...

(Begins to spray and wipe imaginary glass on her right side.)

Housewife: (While working) This is my living room, you see...All glass...The furniture... (Points to imaginary furniture)...And even the rug...This rug is transparent fiberglass... Oh, very comfy....

(Touches imaginary rug with her toe, and then walks in it as if in deep pile carpet.)

Housewife: And I can clean it all, with just a spray and a wipe...

(Sprays imaginary rug and wipes it. Sprays imaginary couch and wipes it. Stands up and looks around at other imaginary furniture, and then to audience.)

Housewife: Isn't that just great? All finished, thanks to this... (Giggles slightly, looks a bit sheepish as if she is keeping a secret)...You know, I bet you're thinking... Asking yourselves sort of... How do I keep from bumping into a glass

Contd.

Housewife: (Continuing) wall when it's so clean... Or from tripping over the couch here... (Motions to couch) ...Well, it's habit I guess... I mean after you live in one of these places for a while, you get the feeling of it...(Thinking)... Mostly, it's *faith*, I guess... I mean I know that there will always be an *up* (Taps an imaginary ceiling)...And a *down*...

(Stomps on the floor.)

Housewife: And a front...

(Taps on front wall. Knocking sound accompanies every tap.)

Housewife: And a *back*...

(Walks back and taps on the back wall, carefully avoiding the imaginary couch as she goes.)

Housewife: All very logical... I mean, that's enough for me... Really, it's kind of nice... This house... Airconditioned and heated and...(Motions around) Plenty of sunlight...(Pauses) Not much privacy, though... That's probably why George and I don't have any children... To have children, you need *privacy*... (Giggles slyly at her own joke)...George decided he liked this house because he likes to stay sort of *in touch* with the world... And those old wood walls, like our neighbors have (Motions to right and left)...Well, in addition to being a fire hazard... They shut out all the world... George says he gets enough privacy at the office, and that when he comes home, he wants to put on a show... But the neighbors are pretty cooperative, I'll have to say that...

Contd.

Housewife: (Continuing) They pull their curtains... And you only need one set of curtains pulled... If you see what I mean... I mean isn't that a little silly when neighbors side by side both pull their curtains?... I mean that's almost wasteful...

(Sees another dirty spot on front wall. Reaches high standing on tiptoes. Sprays and wipes.)

Housewife: (To Audience) Didn't see that one, did you?... So we like it here, George and I do... I suppose you'd call us ordinary in most ways... My mother raised me to be content and have faith that up was up and down was down, and as long as you're inside you're... OK...You know where you stand... I mean I certainly know where I stand...

Housewife

(Taps the right and left walls. Gives the OK sign with index finger and thumb together.)

Housewife: Right in the middle of my home... and anything that's outside...that (eyes grow big) whatever it is out there... (Pauses.. Shakes her head)... Well, it's not airconditioned, anyway...I mean (Earnestly) that is a sobering thought... Did you ever realize that eternity is not airconditioned? ...Just step outside your door...(Self-assured) You'll get a blast of hot or cold... Or rain or snow... We know where we stand, George and I do...And we like it here...

(Sits on the imaginary rug. Feels the luxury of the rug with her spread hand.)

Housewife: My, I love a soft rug... (Stares upward) It wasn't always this way, though... I mean I wasn't too content when I was

Contd.

Housewife: (Continued) young... I was a little hellion, really. . .And my mother used to spank me? Whew!... Always because I'd ask her why... You see... I'd be out at night playing in the grass or climbing up in a tree and watching the stars from the highest limb... Kind of thinking that sometimes the stars might get me and take me away... You know how kids think... And my mother would call from the house and say: "Kerry, you come inside now." ...Because that's my name, Kerry, you see... And she'd say "Kerry, you come in here!" and I'd say (Smiles in reminiscence)..."Why?" ...And she'd say "Cause you got no business up in that tree, looking out at the sky!" ...And I'd say "Why not?"... And then she'd get mad, standing there under the tree, way down there...And she'd shout up at me "Kerry, you're gonna get whipped when you come down!"... And I'd say "Why?" "Cause only <u>crazy</u> people sit up in trees like that!" "Why?" ...And she'd say "I'm not arguing any more, but when you come down I'll get you and whip you!"...

(Lies on her back, relaxing on the imaginary rug.)

Housewife: Well, I always came down because I was hungry and she had the food... So when I got down I'd get the whipping first and the food second... And pretty soon I got tired of being whipped, and just stayed in my house and took the food... I don't know where it ends at first... Being a kid...I guess it ended when I decided to stay in the house and not go up the tree...(Thinking) I always felt a little guilty, I think, because I stopped asking why and just ate my food...

Contd.

Housewife: (Continuing) ...(Quickly) But I can put that guilt out of my mind now, because I've got a house of my very own...And I like staying inside... I really do...Only (hesitantly)... Every once in a while I feel guilty about stopping asking why... But only occasionally when...

(Stops for a moment as if she has heard a noise. She sits up and looks around the contours of the imaginary room she has created.)

Housewife: (Warily) There's something I didn't tell you about this house... (Looks shiftily sideways)...Something that happens just every so often... When I think about how I stopped asking why... Well...I had good reasons... I mean I didn't want to be spanked, and I wanted to eat, and I didn't want to be crazy... I mean those are good reasons...

(Rises and looks around her very warily.)

Housewife: (Shouting at imaginary walls, frantically) They're good reasons!... (Relaxes slightly) But still sometimes I feel guilty...and that's when... What I have to tell you about this house... Well, I always take care of it before George comes home... Ah! (Looking at right wall) Another spot...

(Sprays spot on the imaginary glass wall and wipes. Then looks suspiciously at glass. Then to audience.)

Housewife: Does that wall look like it's in the same place to you? (Looks again, Taps) ...I'm not sure...It might be... What I was telling you about...

(Taps front wall and then moves to tap side wall.)

Contd.

Housewife: (Shrugging) Maybe it's just my imagination...(More assured)...I think it is... This new spray gets the walls so clean that sometimes my imagination starts working on me... It shouldn't... I mean I really do have faith in up and down and left (Taps left wall)...and...

(Moves very cautiously to the right wall. And taps. The imaginary walls have moved closer together.)

Housewife: ...and right...(Draws back with a small gasp)...Listen...(Looks at audience) ...What I was telling you about these walls...(Taps suspiciously above her head)...and the ceiling...

(With the movements of a caged rodent, she taps the front and then runs to tap the back wall. They, too, have moved much closer together.)

Housewife: ...and front and back, too... They are still there, but...

(She is befuddled, looking away from the audience, but turns slowly towards audience as the realization comes upon her. She fixes the audience with a menacing stare, which she holds several seconds and then explodes.)

Housewife: (Angrily) Why did you get me to tell you that?...About feeling guilty about not asking why...

(Checks the position of all walls and the ceiling now as she talks, with a touch but no knock. The walls are now only within one step of her reach and she can touch the ceiling without going on tiptoes. Her talk stops and she looks out at audience in a less angry sort of manner.)

Housewife: You knew...(Points her finger) You knew... You knew all about my house... My walls...

(Puts fingers up against imaginary front glass as if pressing and almost snarls at audience.)

Housewife: And you knew what it would do to me...

Contd.

(Moves back from glass and looks very suspiciously at each wall in turn and then back at audience.)

Housewife: And now it's happening. . .(Angrily again). . .Are you happy?... (Mocking) Are you happy because it's happening to me this time?. . .I thought you were my friends. . . I really thought so... I wouldn't have told you about feeling guilty if I didn't think you were my friends. . .(Pauses). . .Well...You don't get friends, ever. . . All you get are.. .Spectators. . .

(Reaches out to touch walls again. They are just out of arms reach. She barely has to lean in either direction to touch them.

Housewife: (To herself softly) Oh my God... (To audience). . .Well I hope you like your show. . . You paid for it with trust. . . Do you think I'll ever trust people like you again?. . .Or any people?

(Now she can touch all walls without moving from her spot on center stage. She holds both arms stretched out to the sides and gives the effect of the walls slowly pushing in on her fingers. Pulls arms in quickly, repulsed by the approaching walls.)

Housewife: Looking wildly at audience) But I'm not crazy. . . A little guilty maybe... But not crazy. . . I never ask why anymore. . .but I know my ups...

(Taps ceiling, which is just above her head now.)

Housewife: . . .And downs ...And I'm not crazy... (Pauses) I'm content. . . (Suddenly howls) CONTENT!

(The ceiling seems to press her head down into her shoulders, her two hands flat against the incoming walls, her arms bending slightly... Slowly she seems forced into a crucifix position, pushing out against the imaginary walls. Her tilted head, pushed by the imaginary ceiling, stares violently out at the audience...)

Contd.

Housewife: (Shouting) Damn you! Damn you all!... I'm CONTENT!

Lights Black

End

Floor Plan and Production Notes

In end, thrust, or proscenium stage the actress works mainly against an imaginary front wall and imaginary side walls to a lesser extent. She and the audience "create"the closing house.

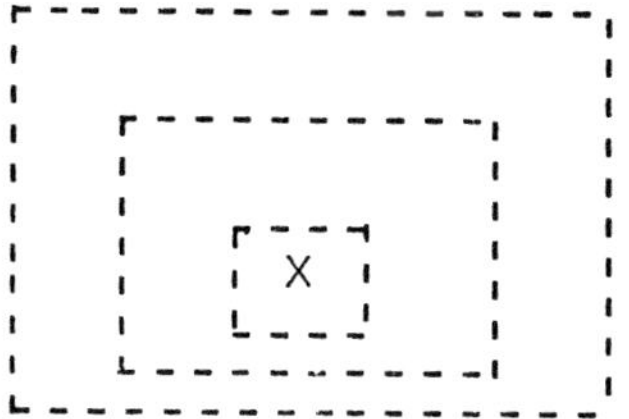

In the round, the actress must consider herself less attached to the front window and must play all four windows equally.

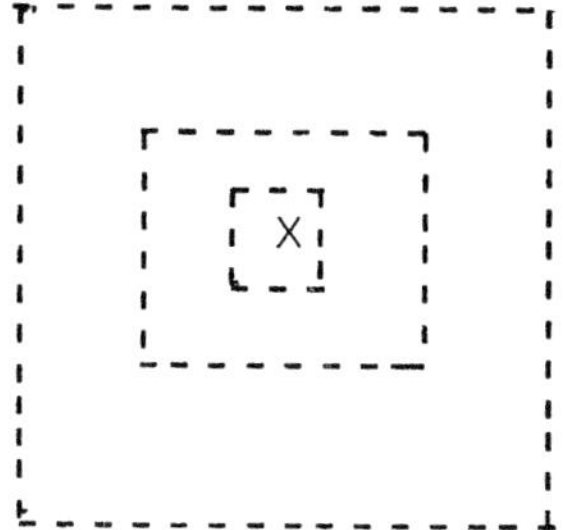

The play deals with howWestern Man is tied to a logical contentment. There are numerous philosophical treatises on this, but in Glass Houses I attempt to portray rather than explain this phenomenon. Contentment, if worshipped, can be claustrophobic. Witness our cities and the increasing neuroses of city dwellers.

The knocking sounds on the imaginary glass are not absolutely necessary to the play and because of intense coordination needed between actress and offstage knocker, this portion can easily be dispensed with. In its place however, must come much more control by the actress, fingertip control reacting to the imaginary touch of closing walls, and mainly audience control, because if there is not so much as a knocker offstage, the communication becomes as direct as it can be in the theatre situation.

Props needed? A window bottle and a rag.

War Surplus

a one-act play

by David C. Hon

Cast of Characters

The Lieutenant) Krosky) Top Sergeant) Corporal) Station Manager) Delivery Man)	This progression of characters can be played by two actors donning different clothing
Dad Mom Sis	Middle-class American family

(WS)

(Two men in battle uniform huddle behind chairs a short distance apart. Sounds of shells bursting. The Lieutenant is talking on his radio.)

Lieutenant: (Almost bored) This is Dago Red. Please get this straight this time... I want artillery to hit the *enemy*, see... I gave my position to you so you would know where *not* to shoot, see...(Perturbed) *And* you went and fired at my position... Right... That's right, you dropped all those shells right on top of us. Now that's not very *American*, is it?

(More sounds of shellbursts. Some laughter in the distance.)

Lieutenant: Yes, those were your shells... but it's not the shells I mind so much. I can take a few shells... I just hate to have the *enemy* sitting out there *laughing* at *us*...

(Offstage laughter, hyena-like)

Lieutenant: So fix it, OK? ...Uh, yeah, me too... Over... *Out*, I mean...Whatever... (Lays radio down and turns to Private Krosky) Krosky?

Krosky: (Looking up as if awakened) Yes sir?

Lieutenant: What do you think we ought to do, Krosky? Should we push on and get butchered or stay here and get butchered?

Krosky : I can't keep holding your hand, sir. You've got to make some of your own decisions.

Contd.

Lieutenant: Yes, yes of course... (Looks befuddled for a moment, then brightens) ...Bring me my comic book.

Krosky: But sir...

Lieutenant: Just bring me my Sergeant Fury comicbook.

Krosky: But it's gone, sir.

Lieutenant: (Really worried) What? My Sgt. Fury comic gone? ...You can't do this to me, Krosky... You know I'm a legend around here, sitting calm and cool with bullets zipping around, reading my comic book...

Krosky: Well sir... It's Collingwood. He borrowed it.

Lieutenant: (Furious) Traitor! Subversive! I give you one job around here, to hold on to my comic book... (Settling down) All right, go get it from Collingwood.

Krosky: There's a problem with that, too... Remember how you told us all to go out and drag back our buddies, no matter what?

Lieutenant: So what about my comic book?

Krosky: Well, Burnett was hit in that clearing by the enemy machine gun, see... and Collingwood was his buddy, see... But the machine gun would get Collingwood easy if he just ran out there, see...

Contd.

Lieutenant: (Irritated) The comic, Krosky... The comic.

Krosky: And Collingwood was so scared that he knew if he tried to crawl out he'd just bury his head in the mud and never get there.

Lieutenant: (Ranting) So what did he do with my comic book?

Krosky: (Almost in tears) So he gritted his teeth and ran out there.

Lieutenant: (Looking out over the top of the chair) Out there?

Krosky: Yes sir.

Lieutenant: (Shaken) And my comic?

Krosky: Ripped to shreds, sir... fifty cal, it was...

Lieutenant: That's a shame... (Dazed) Best I ever had... Sgt. Fury, by damn... (Looks fiercely out) God I hate <u>gooks</u>!

Lights black

(Two men appear in work fatigues - not battle uniform - carrying a coffin-sized box onstage. One man, Top, has several stripes on his arm. The other, Corporal, has only two. They set the box down.)

Top: What's the matter, Corporal... Tired?

Corporal: That's seventeen bodies we've gift-wrapped and thrown in the truck... (Breathing hard) Just let me rest a second...

Top: And this is the last one... Come on, let's get it addressed and up on the truck...

Corporal: (Krinkling nose) Really stinks around here...

Contd.

Top: (Pulling up lid of box) Another one without a tag...oh yeah...here's something...a letter from his folks... (Pulls out envelope, and continues looking in box)...Here we are, a note from his Lieutenant... What's it written on? (Pulls out a strip of comic book, reads from it) Send this body on... Will fill in details for death telegram from this end... (Looking up from note) OK Corporal, address it with the return address from this envelope...

Corporal: But Top, we're supposed to have a receipted death telegram before we ship it.

Top: (Looking shiftily about) You're right, it does stink around here (Holds the letter and writes the address on the top of the box) Collingwood... (Continues writing)

Corporal: We can't just send it on, can we?

Top: You want to stay here and baby sit with it?... (Reassuring) They'll catch up with it at the port... Someone will catch it...

Corporal: But Top...

Top: (Grabbing one end of the box) Come on... this is the last one... We can go wash the stink out of our noses after this one...

(Reluctantly, the Corporal takes his end of the box, and they lift it)

Lights black

(Lights on to two men standing over the box. Station Manager has on a white shirt and wears a green visor. Delivery Man wears a blue work shirt.)

Sta. Man: (Reading off box and writing it on clipboard) Charles Collingwood, 25 Rosemary Lane, Finley, Ohio.

Del. Man: (Tilting box up to look at underside) Military shipment... What's this guy doing, buying war surplus before the war is over?

Contd.

Sta. Man: (Surveying his clipboard still) None of our business. . .

Del. Man: (Grumbling) All these outdoor heroes buying up liferafts and canteens so they can go out and make war on ducks. . .

Sta. Man: (Noncommital) Well, Phil. . . we're just workin' on the railroad, All the live-long day. . .

Del. Man: This thing comes from overseas, too. . . Look at the rubber stamp on the underside (Looks up at Station Manager) They're selling stuff right off the battlefield!

Sta. Man: Well, the Department of Defense knows what they're doin'. . . Their business is to fight wars and ours is to deliver boxes.

Del. Man: (Rising) OK. . . Deliver it, then?

Sta. Man: Yeah. . . Too many boxes cluttering this depot. . . Better get it outta here.

Lights black

(When Lights come on again, box is gone and chairs are arranged in a family scene. Daddy sits reading a newspaper. Mother is looking through a mail-order catalogue. Sis is lying on the floor nearly carressing a telephone receiver as she talks into it.)

Daddy: (To mother) Says here we only lost 43 in combat last week.

Mother: Yes, that's better than the week before. . . The week before we lost 55.

Contd.

Daddy: But the enemy lost 650 last week... (Relaxes) That makes me feel good.

Mother: Yes, and the week before that the enemy only lost 400... The balance is shifting. I just know it is...

Daddy: (Self-satisfied) That's just great... (Rises and goes over to hug Mother) It's just great to know our boy is on a winning team.

Mother: (Reflective) Well... we deserve it... because we're Americans... We certainly deserve to be the winners. (Hugs Daddy)

Sis: (Into the telephone) Why... I could, Jerry... For you I could...

Daddy: (Suspicious) Could what?

Mother: Yes... Could what?

Sis: (Into receiver) Just a minute Jerry ...My parents are living out their sexual fantasies by eavesdropping...

Mother: (Caught in the act) I am not.

Daddy: Could what?

Sis: (To Daddy) Could get my soldier brother to send back an enemy flag... So there.

Daddy: What does he need that for?

Sis: Oh, you know boys... (Covering up the receiver) Daddy this is very important... I've already sent off a letter asking him to send some war souvenirs...

Contd.

Daddy: I don't understand...

Mother: (Nodding) I do...

Sis: (Into receiver) Just one more second Jerry... Don't go 'way... (Covering receiver again) Daddy Jerry's probably going to be the high scorer on the basketball team... and...well... this will help me... get him.

Daddy: (Seeing the light) Ah... Tell him sure... Tell him your brother can even get him an enemy bullet for a souvenir.

Sis: (Brightening) Really? (Into phone) Jerry, Daddy says my brother can even get you an enemy bullet... Cross my heart and hope to die... That's right... (Listening) Saturday night... after the game...yes...uh (To parents) I can go out with Jerry after the game Saturday, huh Mom? Dad?

(Mother and Daddy beam at each other)

Daddy: Certainly.

Sis: (Into phone) Gee that would be great, Jerry... OK, I'll see you then... (Lovingly) Bye Jerry...

Mother: (Pointing to a page in the catalogue) See? ...It will be just like that... My new sofa.

Daddy: (Perplexed) Doesn't have any back.

Mother: It's not suppose to have any back. New style, very chic ...

Contd.

Daddy: (Shrugging) Well... If it's already ordered.

Sis: (Gazing into space) I wrote him a month ago... Asking if he'd send me a box of flags and stuff...

Mother: You did?

Sis: Yeah... (Enthusiastically) Best thing yet for getting dates... except I better produce something pretty soon, or it's back to the back seat of the car...

(Mother and Daddy beam and hug again, delighted with their daughter's cleverness)

Daddy: Well, it will probably be here soon... which reminds me, I'm expecting a large war surplus tent for my fishing trips... Wonder when *it* will get here?

Mother: The way shipping is nowadays, we'll all be lucky if we *ever* see what we ordered.

(The Delivery Man drags the box onstage.) He knocks on the door and waits. Daddy goes to the door.)

Daddy: Yes?... (Sees box) Oh *yes*...

Del.Man: Want to sign for this?

Daddy: (Fumbling for pen) Uh yes... Who's it from?

Del.Man: (Handing over a pen and the receipt pad) Don't know... Not our business.

Daddy: (Signing, handing back pad and looking over the box) Wooden box...

Contd.

Daddy: (Continuing) Pretty well made... (To Del.Man) Well, thank you...

(Delivery Man nods, waits for a tip.)

Daddy: Uh yes... (Fumbles out some change) Well thank you again...

Del.Man: (Looking disgusted at meager tip) No wonder you buy war surplus...

Daddy: (Annoyed) Thank you. ..

Del.Man: (Throwing hand up in quick motion as he leaves, mumbling) Break my back, strain my guts out for these people...

(Exit Del.Man)

Sis: (Coming to Daddy's side) Oh he did send some things.,. Oh it's a big box... If there are guns and flags and bullets... Oh, I'll never have to worry about dates... (Playacts) Thank you for the nice time Jerry... Here's your bullet... (Withholds imaginary bullet) ...Jerry, aren't you going to try to kiss me? ...Two bullets if you kiss me, Jerry... (Closes her eyes in ecstasy, puckers lips) Ooooo... That was a three bullet kiss...

Daddy: Nonsense... This is my fishing tent... (Examining box)... But I can't see how to get this box open... Going to need a hammer.

(Daddy exits as mother comes running in)

Mother: (Hysterical) Oh, my sofa from Sears... God bless them... Oh, how nice... I just ordered it day before yesterday... (Almost in tears) I'll never say a bad word about Sears again.

Contd.

Sis: (Defiantly) That's not a Sears box... That's my bullets and flags.

Mother: (Still hysterical, swooning not listening) Oh I had so hoped it would be here for my Saturday tea party... And Oh goodness... I just hoped against hope... and here it is!

(Daddy returns with hammer)

Daddy: War surplus always takes a long time, but you get great values... (Starts banging on box)

Sis: (Over Daddy's shoulder) Careful Daddy... Don't break anything... I don't want to give Jerry a broken gun... (Aside to Mother) If he asks me out again, I'll give him a gun... For a gun he'd love me...

Mother: (Resolutely) No...I'm sorry, but it's my sofa... It's just the right size for my sofa... Oh they'll be so envious, those biddies... Always shuffling around as if I don't have anything to sit on... But my new sofa...Oh... (Holding hands prayer fashion) Bless...oh, God bless Sears...

Daddy: (Prying up lid, which tilts facing audience, obscuring the inside of box) Well, here goes... Got to hand it to them... They sure pack surplus well...

(The whole family gathers around as Daddy lifts the lid. There is a very long silence as they look inside. Then they look very slowly at each other and then back at what lies in the box)

Mother: (Suddenly) I'm going to call Sears right now... They have no business doing this to me.

(Exit Mother)

Contd.

Sis: (Scrutinizing the whole inside of the box) There doesn't seem to be a gun or a flag anywhere... (Backing away)... What will I tell Jerry? ...(Beginning to cry) What will I tell him now?

Daddy: (Putting his arm around Sis, speaking philosophically) Well now...there, there... When you live as long as I have, you know none of us get exactly what we want exactly when we want it... I wanted that surplus equipment very badly, and you see how long they've taken... But don't cry... Let me see here... (Reaches in and wrenches around with right hand) There... There you are, (Holds up a large bullet) You can give that to Jerry.

Sis: (Eyeing the bullet keenly, taking it reverently) Oh Daddy... Gee! (She is speechless)

(Enter Mother)

Mother: (Huffy) Those Sears people... They say it will be at least a week....

Daddy: (Preoccupied, pawing through box) I guess I could use these army clothes on fishing trips... Yes, I believe we wore the same size boots, too... (Looking at Mother) Every cloud has a silver lining... Actually, I really needed some boots and some old kick-around clothes.

Mother: (Left out) But what about *me*? My sofa... Oh, I *wanted* it *so*...

Daddy: (Rising, examining the sides of the box) Well... You know... This is a rather nice box... If I just stain the wood, and put foam rubber on the top and cover it with upholstery...

Contd.

Mother: (Becoming excited) Oh, that would be lovely... A sofa and... a utility box... Oh my... (Stepping back to imagine, adoring the box) Oh yes... (Then looking admiringly at Daddy) You are such a wonderful husband.

(Sis and Mother hugging Daddy from both sides, Daddy beaming, hugging both of them, all standing behind the open box, facing the audience as if for a family picture)

Sis: (Fondling her bullet)...And such a wonderful Daddy....

(All smiles, hold pose)

Lights black

End

Floor Plan and Production Notes

This play can be done on any type of stage. It has four scenes which, on a large stage could occupy separate lighting areas.

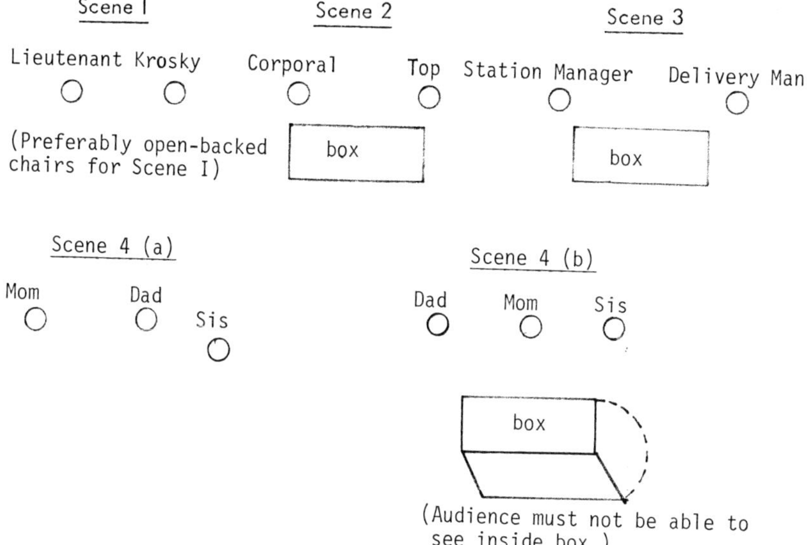

War Surplus depends first upon three rapidly paced scene changes. If only five actors are used then costume changes must be rapid. The way it has been performed so far, the Lieutenant also plays Corporal and Station Manager, Daddy plays Top, and Krosky plays the Delivery Man. The audience will buy this if the actors change both costume and character.

When the box is open an unusually long pause is very effective. If the audience has been attentive up to that point, a dead stillness falls and up to forty-five seconds have been used, during which all the evils of modern man and his war rush out intangibly to fill the theatre and grip the proceedings. The actors must remain nearly motionless for this time and Mommy must finally break the pause incisively with no telegraphing beforehand.

Airplane

a one-act play by

David C. Hon

Cast of Characters

Pilot

Copilot

Madman

Stewardess

Priest

Mother

Little Girl

Old Woman

Time - Present

Setting - A small airplane travelling between insignificant cities.

(AP) !

(The stage is blank except for several ordinary chairs arranged in the manner seats are in a DC-3 aircraft. The seats of the Pilot and Copilot are set slightly apart and to the left on the stage, with the rest of the side view of the airplane continuing behind to the right. To the far right, in the rear of the airplane, is a small chamberpot, if possible, a toilet stool. The Pilot is speaking into an imaginary microphone in his hand and the passengers are listening.)

Pilot: This will be a short flight tonight, probably only half an hour if we have our usual tail wind. We welcome you to our airline, and if you need anything, just ask our stewardess.

(The Stewardess is standing between the Pilot's seat and the seats of the passengers. She smiles and nods.)

Mother: (Sitting three seats back on the aisle, admonishes her daughter, the Little Girl who is in a window seat) You can't ask her *that*!

Little Girl: But mother, I need to know. I have my calculations. (The Little Girl shows her mother a slide rule.)

Mother: I will not permit it. You cannot ask her that. And she probably does not know how long it would take us to fall to the ground.

Little Girl: I will ask her how high we are, and then I can calculate the rest.

Mother: All right. But do not tell her the reason. (Woman holds up her hand to the Stewardess.)

Contd.

Stewardess: May I help you?

Mother: My daughter wants to know ...

Little Girl: (Interrupting) How high are we?

Stewardess: I'm not certain . (Smiling) Let me ask the Pilot. (Starts toward the front of the airplane.)

Pilot: (Talking to Copilot) It's boring now, you know.

Copilot: (Shrugging) It's a way to make money.

Pilot: But in the old days when I learned to fly, there was some danger. Now I feel like a ... lifeguard, or a night-watchman. You are young. You don't remember.

Copilot: I was only a boy during the war. But I understand why it is boring for you. After flying fighter planes in the war, this is nothing ... I know, I saw all the movies.

Stewardess: (Pretending to open an imaginary door to the cockpit, and leaning her head in, scowling) Excuse me. A little girl wants to know how high we are flying.

Copilot: She'll probdbly get sick when you tell her.

Pilot: Tell her fifteen thousand feet and give her a plastic bag.

Priest: (Sitting next to the window, talking to Madman)

Contd.

Priest: (Continued) No, we are not nearer to God up here. God is everywhere.

Madman: Not even a *little* nearer?

Priest: (Shaking head) Not even a little.

Madman: That's good.

Priest: Why?

Madman: (Looking suspicious) I don't know ... I don't know why I said that.

Stewardess: (Coming back with the plastic bag behind her back, to Little Girl) We are flying at fifteen thousand feet. (Smiling her false smile) Do you feel sick?

Little Girl: I just asked how high we are.

Stewardess: But sometimes that makes little girls sick.

Little Girl: I'm tired of people asking me if I'm sick. Do I look sick?

Mother: Don't talk like that to the nice lady.

Little Girl: Maybe the nice lady is sick. Why are you holding that bag behind you? Are you going to be sick?

Stewardess: (Still trying to be pleasant) No. But sometimes little girls get sick.

Contd.

Little Girl: Your smile is sick. Why don't you put that bag over your head?

Mother: (Embarrassed) I'm sorry. My daughter is not behaving like a young lady ... I'm very sorry. Thank you for telling us how high we are.

Stewardess: (Still forcing a smile) Certainly.

Madman: (Leaning back to Stewardess) Have you got a napkin?

Stewardess: Certainly. (Goes to the rear and brings a napkin) Anything else?

Madman: No thank you.

Stewardess: If you are blowing your nose, we have special tissues for that.

Madman: No, I'm not blowing my nose.

Stewardess: (A little curious) If you are sick, we have special bags.

Madman: No, I'm not sick.

Stewardess: If you have a spot on your clothing, we have special cleaning material.

Madman: Oh? Perhaps you *can* help me then. I want to clean my gun. (He takes a large, heavy pistol out of his coat.)

Stewardess: (Surprised and a little frightened) But you are not permitted to have a gun on this airplane.

Contd.

Madman: Why not?

Stewardess: It says that in the rules.

Madman: I didn't read the rules.

Stewardess: I'll have to ask you to give me your gun. I will give it to you when we land.

Madman: But I need it now. Why can't I keep it?

Stewardess: Because it says that in the rules. Now please give me the gun.

Madman: (Shaking his head) I need this gun. I need it now and always ... Maybe you ought to ask the pilot to change the rules, just this time.

Stewardess: (Frustrated) Why don't you give me the gun?

Madman: Why don't you ask the pilot?

Stewardess: (Very nervous) Yes, of course. I'll ask the pilot. (Stewardess moves to the front).

Old Lady: (Stopping the Stewardess) What is that young man doing with that gun?

Stewardess: He's just cleaning it.

Old Lady: Is he a policeman?

Stewardess: No ... (shaking her head, confused) No, he's just a man with a gun ... Please excuse me ...

Contd.

Stewardess: (Continued) (She pretends to lean her head in the imaginary cockpit door) Excuse me, but...

Pilot: (Smiling) Did she get sick?

Stewardess: No ... This is important. A man back there has a gun and he won't give it to me.

Copilot: Why do you need a gun?

Stewardess: I don't, but it says in the rules. It says: No firearms are permitted. This man told me to ask you to change the rule.

Copilot: Is he a bandit?

Stewardess: I don't know. But I know the rules say ...

Pilot: Yes, I know the rules . . . Well, lock the door here and hide your key. Then tell him that I will not change the rules, and that he will have problems with the police if he doesn't give you his gun.

Stewardess: (Gulping) He won't like that.

Pilot: Well, lock the door. If he is harmless, he will give you the gun. If he is dangerous, we will land very soon and the police will be waiting.

Copilot: Do you want me to help her?

Pilot: No, if he shoots through the door he will probably hit one of us. The stewardess can handle him. (To Stewardess) Keep contact by the telephone in the back.

Contd.

Stewardess: (Gulping again) Okay. (She closes the door, and locks it.)

Copilot: (To Pilot) You seem happy.

Pilot: (Smiling) Life is boring without danger.

Copilot: You can relax the rules.

Pilot: But then, if he robs the passengers, what can I tell the police? I have to say that I tried. Those rules are for the protection of the passengers.

Copilot: But in this case, perhaps the rules make danger.

Pilot: (Smiling) I know.

Madman: (Holding out the dirty napkin to the Stewardess) Thank you. I've cleaned my gun. What did the pilot say?

Stewardess: Just a moment. (Walks to the back of the plane and drops the key in the toilet.)

Priest: (Looking at the gun) What do you do with your gun?

Madman: Nothing.

Old Lady: (From across the aisle) Do you shoot people?

Madman: Not usually.

Priest: There must be something wrong if you have a gun.

Madman: Why?

Contd.

Old Lady: Because normal people don't need guns.

Priest: *I* don't have a gun.

Madman: You have God.

Priest: Anyone can have God.

Old Lady: Yes, that's right. Anyone can have God.

Madman: No, I have to have this gun.

Stewardess: (Returning) Well, I'm sorry, but the pilot says he will not change the rules.

Madman: Well, I'm sorry too, but I'm not going to give you my gun.

Stewardess: Do you *really* need it?

Madman: Do you?

Stewardess: Well, no. . . But the rules say I must have the gun.

Madman: But I *do* need the gun. So the rules *are* absurd.

Stewardess: But *why* do you need it?

Priest: Yes, why?

Old Lady: Yes, why?

Madman: (Hesitating) Because of power. Everybody has some kind of power, and I want some, too.

Stewardess: Please give me the gun. You don't need the power here . . . (Holds her hand out for the gun.)

Contd.

Madman: I do! (Draws the gun to his chest) I need it everywhere.

Old Lady: But we don't have power.

Madman: Yes you do. You all have power enough. The Priest has power. The stewardess has power. The pilot has power. Even that woman (Points to the Mother behind) . . . she has power over her little girl, and her little girl has power because she is a helpless child . . . And I, I need my power.

Old Lady: I don't have power.

Madman: Yes, you do. Age has power. People respect age.

Stewardess: (Pleading) Please give me the gun.

Madman: (Standing up) I won't. (He appears crazy) You want my power and yours, too. And you can't have it. (Points the gun at her.)

Stewardess: (Backing away) I just don't want . . . trouble. (Backs to the last seat in the aisle.)

Madman: (Waving gun) All of you . . . All of you want to take my power away.

Old Lady: The police will be waiting when we land . . . (Righteously) <u>They'll</u> take your power away.

Madman: (Considering) Not if we fly

Contd.

Madman: (Continued) to somewhere far away. I'll tell the pilot to fly far away. (He tries the cockpit door. It is locked.)

Stewardess: (Talking from behind a seat on a small telephone) He's pointing his gun at us.

Pilot: What does he want?

Stewardess: Power.

Pilot: What kind of power?

Stewardess: I don't know. Simply <u>power</u> . . . Just a minute, he's coming back to me . . . (Puts the receiver under her seat quickly)

Madman: You have the key . . . I saw you take the key. Where is it?

Stewardess: (Pointing to the rest-room) In there.

Madman: (Pretending to open imaginary door and looking into the toilet) In there?

Stewardess: In there.

Madman: Why did you do that?

Stewardess: It seemed like a good place for a key.

Madman: (As to a friend) Do you think the pilot will open the door if I knock?

Stewardess: Maybe he will..

Contd.

(Madman goes toward the front. Again the Stewardess picks up the telephone.)

Stewardess: He's going back up front. He wants to knock on your door.

(Madman knocks)

Pilot: I hear him.

Copilot: We don't want any, whatever it is.

Pilot: (To Copilot) I have a way to get that gun from him. I'll do a trick with the airplane.

Copilot: (Wary) What kind of trick?

Pilot: A loop. I did loops many times in the war. If he is standing up he will fall upside down. But it's dangerous. I'll wait a few minutes.

Copilot: This isn't boring, is it?

Pilot: (Smiling, talking to the Stewardess in his telephone) Listen . . . I'm going to tell the people to fasten their seat belts because of bad weather. Try to persuade him to continue standing. In reality, I'm going to make a loop.

Stewardess: I'll try.

Pilot: (Into another imaginary microphone) This is the pilot speaking. We are going to have some rough weather now. Please fasten your seat belts.

Contd.

(All of the passengers fasten their seatbelts. The Madman, standing, seems confused.)

Stewardess: (To Madman) You ought to sit down and fasten your seatbelt, too.

Madman: (Frantically) No! It's a trick. You just want to show your power over me. Well I'm not going to sit down. Ha!

Priest: (Fatherly) No one is going to hurt you.

Old Lady: Why do you need so much power?

Madman: To be free. To be equal. If I don't have power, I am nothing. I just want to be equal.

Priest: But we are all equal under God's power.

Madman: Not me. I'm at the bottom. I haven't even got enough power without this gun to be equal to anybody. People won't let me be equal. But with this gun, they let me.

Priest: But without it?

Madman: Without it, I am nothing.

Priest: No one is nothing.

Madman: Wrong. Without this power I am nothing.

Little Girl: What's wrong with being nothing?

Contd.

Madman: (Considering her statement an intelligent one) I really don't like power so much, you know. It's very artificial.

Mother: Well, then why don't you give the Stewardess your gun.

Madman: (Frantic again) Because then she would have all my power.

Madman: (Continuing) Right now, in this moment, I am free, because I have more power than I have ever had in my life. See? (Points the gun at the Old Lady) The Old Lady is afraid. (Laughs)

Old Lady: (Quivering) Of course I'm afraid.

Madman: (Turning to the Mother) See? (Points the gun) This mother is afraid.

Mother: You must be crazy.

Stewardess: (Into the telephone) He's pointing his gun at the passengers. Maybe he is going to shoot someone.

Pilot: Okay. Get ready.

Madman: (Continuing) But I don't like it. I don't like to use this gun. If I could be free, if no one had power over me, I would not need power. I would like to be free without my gun, but this is better than nothing.

Pilot: Here goes. (Pushes the imaginary

Contd.

Pilot: (Continued) wheel in. Everyone in the airplane leans forward. The Madman falls backward grabbing the top of a seat. The Pilot speaks to his Copilot.) Did I ever tell you about shooting at trains during the war? (He seems very happy.)

Copilot: (In a cool manner) We are going down very quickly.

Pilot: I know. This is the first part of a loop.

Copilot: I'm glad this is a DC-3. It's ugly, but it's strong.

Madman: (Shouting, holding his gun out) I've still got my power. You can't make me afraid.

Little Girl: (Working her slide rule) If our angle is 45 degrees, we are only 2000 feet above the ground. We will crash in 30 seconds.

Stewardess: (Into telephone) The little girl says we will crash in thirty seconds.

Pilot: She's right. Here we go . . . <u>up</u>! (Pulls the imaginary wheel toward him.

(Everyone in the plane leans back and the plane seems to climb rapidly. The Madman stumbles back to the rear of the plane, and holds onto the seat by the Stewardess.)

Stewardess: (Smiling falsely) Are you certain you would not like to sit down and fasten your seatbelt?

Contd.

Madman: No! I won't give him power . . . (Struggles up to the front, and beats on the cockpit door, shouting) I won't give you power!

Priest: Bad weather is God's power.

Madman: I won't give him power, either.

(Mother, Priest, and Old Lady all gasp.)

Pilot: (Into telephone) Here we go . . . around!

(Certain people toss things in the air. The women scream. Everyone holds onto the seats of their chairs. The Madman at first clings to a seat and then does a handstand and crumples to the floor. His gun goes flying down the aisle, and the Stewardess calmly picks it up as everyone relaxes breathless in the seats.)

Mother: This certainly is rough weather!

(The Stewardess walks to the toilet with the gun and drops it in.)

Madman: (Weakly struggling to his feet) My gun! Where is my gun?

Little Girl: (Pointing to the back) It went that way.

Pilot: (First into his telephone) Did he lose his gun?

Stewardess: (Into telephone) Yes, I disposed of it.

Pilot: That's good . . . (He is laughing with relief as he speaks into an imaginary microphone in his hand) This is your Pilot speaking . . . We had a little rough weather

Contd.

Pilot: (Continued) but now we are resuming our normal altitude and we anticipate no more problems. Thank you for your cooperation. (Puts down the imaginary microphone.)

Copilot: I'll bet that little girl is sick now.

Madman: (Running back to Stewardess) Where's my gun? Did you see my gun come this way?

Stewardess: Yes.

Madman: Where is it?

Stewardess: (Pointing to the toilet) In there.

Madman: (Dismayed) In there?

Stewardess: (Nodding) In there.

Madman: Why is everything important in there?

Stewardess: It seems to be the best place for many things.

Little Girl: Including stories about airplanes . . .

Madman: (Raging back up the aisle) But what about my power? Now I'm *nothing*!

Priest: We are all nothing in God's power.

Madman: I didn't want that gun anyway. I just wanted to be free.

Contd.

Old Lady: No one is free of God's power.

Priest: He decides when we will die.

Madman: (Raging like an animal) Oh, no. You're wrong. Wrong, wrong, WRONG!

Priest: No, I know that fact absolutely.

Madman: And now . . . Ha ha . . . I will demonstrate my power over you, because I am right and you are wrong and . . . (he walks to the back of the plane) . . . I will also demonstrate my power . . . (He twists open the imaginary door of the aircraft) . . . over God . . . I will be . . . (He jumps) . . . Freeeeeee . . . (He jumps off the stage into the audience, his arms outspread as if he is falling free.)

Stewardess: My god! (She jumps up and looks after him in amazement, and after a few moments pulls the door shut. Everyone is turning in their seats, gaping.)

Mother: (Hiding her little girl's eyes) He went into the rest room.

Little Girl: (Nonchalantly taking out her slide rule) You never tell me the truth, mother, so I never listen. The rest room is on the other side, and that man is now falling at 32 feet per second squared.

Stewardess: (Into telephone) He jumped.

Pilot: (To Copilot) He jumped.

Contd.

Copilot: (Looking out his side window) He should have good visibility tonight. The stars are very clear.

Pilot: Out of my plane. He jumped out of my plane. This won't look good. (Into telephone) Can you take him off the passenger list?

Stewardess: (Looking at her clipboard) He wasn't on it.

(Directly into front of the audience, the Madman stands. His arms are outspread, and there is an exhalted expression on his face.)

Madman: I'm free . . . The stars, the earth, the sky . . . They are all _mine_. . . I am _power_ . . . I am _free_!

(The Little Girl inside the plane is furiously working her slide rule and looking at her watch.)

Little Girl: Thirty-two feet per second times thirty-two feet per second times fifteen thousand feet . . . He's about halfway down now.

Priest: (Shaking his head) He was right . . . (To the Old Lady) He was right and I was wrong.

Madman: It's cold . . . (Holds himself and shivers) But look . . . oh, look at the lights . . . the little lights on the cars on the highway. . . I'm over a road . . . It's my road . . . They're my cars . . . Just like a Christmas with my toys . . . And now they're coming right up to me . . . It's wonderful, wonderful . . . to be . . . .

Contd.

Little Girl: (In monotone) He will be landing . . . (Looking at her watch) Just about . . . now . . .

Madman: (A look of satisfaction on his face) Free!

(Instant lights out)

(Curtain)

End

Floor Plan and Production Notes

Whether in the round or not Airplane should be set up with sixteen chairs set up in as elongated a fashion as possible. Seating positions are as numbered. (Only Madman and Stewardess leave their seats).

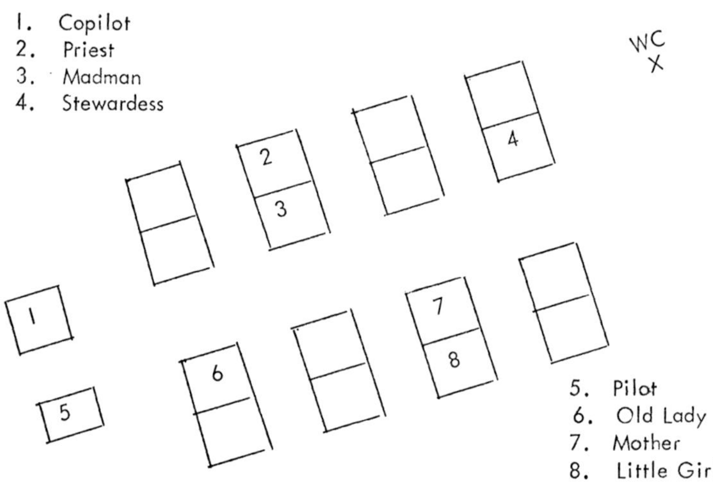

Airplane is obviously a parody not only on a popular movie but also on the whole airplane/passenger milieu, on the vagaries of power and those who maintain it, and on the concept of freedom which may never quite fully be discussed.

Airplane is a director's piece, requiring pace and timing, especially when the plane does its loop. There the exhilaration of movement should be transmitted to the audience as the players lean forward and backward in unison.

The Stewardess runs the show in effect because her insistence on the rules drives the action. Therefore all things naturally revolve around the performance of this rather "plastic" character.

Beat the Press

a one-act play by

David C. Hon

Cast of Characters

Moderator
Lily Lyons
Trumbull Mortenson
Mary Contrary
Senator Wallaby Thump

(BP)

(Play opens with a Moderator dressed in suit ready to begin at air time. Three reporters wait in chairs: Lily Lyons, Trumbull Mortenson, and Mary Contrary.)

Moderator: (To audience) Welcome once again to Beat the Press, the weekly public affairs program dedicated to illuminating the issues and to questioning the men so involved in these issues. Our correspondents this week are Lily Lyons of the Philadelphia Gong (Pauses while Lily Lyons smiles to the audience), Trumbull Mortenson of the River City Gazette, and Mary Contrary of the Atlanta Messenger. Without further ado I will introduce our guest and we can. . . (Smiles to reporters). . . Have at him.

(Reporters bounce up and down on their seats in anticipation.)

Moderator: Our esteemed guest today is the junior senator from Oklahoma, a young man whom congressional leaders call "on the move". His party has great things in store for him, so let's see what he has on his mind. . . Let us welcome Senator Wallaby Thump. . .

(Round of applause from reporters and moderator as Thump walks on stage. He scrutinizes the face of each reporter at close range before he takes his seat.)

Moderator: Good day, Senator Thump.

(Senator Thump nods, smiles, takes his seat.)

Moderator: You know this group of reporters already.

(Thump nods regretfully.)

Moderator: (A bit nonplussed at Thump's silence, hurries) And so let us begin the questioning. . .

Contd.

(Lily Lyons raises hand.)

Moderator: Miss Lyons.

Lyons: (Briskly) Senator Thump, you recently said that "unless the economy gets back on its feet it is going nowhere". Could you explain this statement to us a bit more thoroughly? Especially in light of your recent votes for even more deficit spending.

Sen. Thump: (Looks cagily sideways, gulps, takes deep breath, and bursts into song):

I'd like to make this. . . perfectly clear
It's very simple. . . really my dear
Just tell the people. . . they've nothing
to fear
I'd like to make that. . . perfect—ly
clear.

(Everyone is slightly aghast at this, but Lyons, quickly after his last line, snaps back at him.)

Lyons: But that's not really answering the question, Senator Thump. . .

(Rest of reporters grumble in agreement.)

Sen. Thump: (Looking surprised, but twittering into song again)

Well it's really very odious
The things my enemies say
They say I've got no answers
That I can't save the day . . . but

I'd like to make this. . . perfectly clear
The days of prosperity. . . are very near
On this great ship of state, the best men
will steer
(my dear)
I'd like to make that. . . perfect. . . lee
. . . clear.

Contd.

(Moderator and reporters look at each other through half-eyes. Mortenson leans back jauntily, his hand slightly raised.)

Moderator: Mr. Mortenson?

Mortenson: Sen. Thump, though you've gone on record as a big spender, very little of your interest or attention has gone to the people who really need the money, the poor, the jobless. What can you say about that?

Sen. Thump: (Beaming and singing)

Well I'd like to say this about that
We see many poor people grow fat
Yet the masses of poor
Will always want more. . .
I'd like to say this about that.

Mortenson: But Senator Thump. . . Last January you said. . .

Thump: (Continuing same song)

And I'd like to say this about that
I said prosperity can't be bought
And that we could find
Poverty's in the mind
Though we're not doing all that we'd
ought.

(Miss Contrary raises hand.)

Moderator: Miss Contrary?

Contrary: How does that go along with your great friendship with big business. Certainly much of your spending has helped the giant corporations increase their power.

Thump: (Singing logically)

Contd.

Thump: (Continuing)

I don't think you've looked at the
facts
Behind all of my generous acts
If business is strong
Then we'll get along
So I think that you're on the wrong
track.

Contrary: But what about the substantially reduced taxes on big businesses, the ones you proposed last week?

Sen. Thump: (Singing)

Who should pay?
Should it be the very people who
need it?
If this country is to grow
Then we've got to signal go
For the businesses
Which give jobs
Which give products
Which get done
Everything under the sun
Oh. . . We've got to give business
a chance.

Contrary: A chance?

Lyons: A chance?

Mortenson: Then all the taxes will fall on the poor working fellow. . . What about <u>that</u> Senator Thump?

Thump: (Singing cheerily)

Well taxes ought to be as low as
possible I agree,
But often our big country has big
projects don't you see?
There never was a nation that could
find the revelation
To do without its taxes, believe me.

Contd.

Lyons: (Leaning over the table with a malicious look) But most of the taxes are for war. (Squinting) What do you think about war, Senator Thump?

Thump: (Standing with hand over heart)

War. . . is terrible.
War. . . is inexcusable.
War is the wrong thing for anyone to do.

Mortenson: (Not letting up) But you have not suggested we stop doing it. In fact you constantly insist we keep preparing for it. Let me quote. . .

Thump: (Interrupting in song)

War is bad
It might even be called a sin
So the very best thing to do
Is to win.

Contrary: (Shocked) Senator. . . Do you favor war?

Thump: (Singing resolutely)

I never favor war
You may quote me on that score
But if it means the end of
Freedom
Liberty
Equality
Democracy
And all those other things
Then we cannot consider it a sin.
We must go out and win
And the sin is when we bend. . . oh
yes, I say
The sin is not to win.

Mortenson: (Leaning in more closely) And what

Contd.

Mortenson: (Continuing) about our crime rate? What can be done to stop the criminals in our streets? And doesn't the government foster more crime by the treatment of its criminals?

Lyons: (Also leaning in) Yes, what about that?

Contrary: Yes, Senator Thump, what about that?

Thump: (Singing staunchly)

Law and order
We've had it in days gone by
I look back with a sigh. . . (sighs)
On how safe it used to be
I remember perfectly. . .
Now this class of scum
These freaks and bums
Say they'll steal equality
If that's the way it must be
So lets pick up the bricks and mortar
And rebuild our law and order.

(All reporters leaning in viciously. Lyons gets up to his desk and stares into his face.)

Lyons: You are saying nothing, Senator Thump. Not one thing I can write down.

Thump: (Defensively singing)

I beg your pardon
I believe I've answered all your questions
Per---fect--ly.

Mortenson: Saying absolutely nothing, Senator. How about the unemployment problem?

Thump: (Singing very defensively)

Contd.

Thump: (Continuing)
Well we must be realistic
It's only a statistic

Contrary: (Leaning over his desk and growling) The statistics say you've voted against every bill that would create new jobs. . .

Thump: (Leaning away from all the faces) (Singing)

But there's more there than meets the eye
These things must be studies. . . we try
In commissions to weigh out the cost
Against the alternative of what may
be lost. . .

Mortenson: (Very much like an animal, clawing at Thump) And education. . . Why do you always vote against more money for education?

Thump: (Singing, worming out of his chair)

The funds for education are like
Fuzz upon the peach
When what we need are dedicated
Teachers who can teach.

Lyons: (Growling, showing teeth) And that takes money. . . What do you want, a bunch of starving poverty stricken old lady school teachers?

Thump: (Rising, backing against the wall, singing)

You interpret so morosely
You must listen more closely

Contrary: (Fangs showing, clawing) Yes, what about women's rights?

Thump: (Beating them back. He is pressed

Contd.

Thump: [Continued] against the back curtain, singing)

Women have a place in our nation
Like all others
But as mothers
They should know their place in. . .
creation.

(Lyons and Contrary actually leap like lionesses on Thump, Mortenson somewhat back, growling. Thump holds the clawing women back at arm's length.)

Mortenson: And what about pollution?

Thump: (Singing bravely despite fingernails and fangs going for his throat)

I'm glad you asked that question
About all the pollution
I'm sure we must be very close
To finding a solution
Now if you worry when your children
Gag and turn all sickly
Just remember we are trying
To stop pollution quickly.

Mortenson: (Angry) What do you mean quickly? You've done absolutely nothing for four years.

Thump: (Sidestepping, singing melodically)

It takes time
All the problems of living take time
Rome wasn't built
In a day, there's no guilt
Taking time. . . time. . . time.

Lyons: (In absolute killing rage) What about taxes? (Leaps again at Senator Thump, chases him around stage)

Contrary: (Just as furious) And war? (Joins the chase).

Contd.

Thump: (While running, still singing)

But when will you all understand
That the problems of a powerful man
Are many and varied
His whole life is harried
Now when will you all understand?

Mortenson: (Joining the chase) Education!

Contrary: Women's rights!

(Thump, free for a moment, dodges back to grab something. He comes back cracking a small whip once. Everyone stops.)

Thump: There! Ah ha!
Your fangs. . . withdraw.

(Fierce reporters back up, leaning only to snarl and claw.)

Mortenson: Urban renewal!

Lyons: United Nations!

(Thump cracks whip again, grabs stool and chases the three around stage.)

Thump: (Singing bravely) (Cracking whip at each line)

I'll tame you
Refrain you
Contain you
And if you don't like it
I'll maim you.

(Wildly chases reporters around again)

Moderator: (Holding up hands. Everyone stops dead, and listens intently) I'm sorry to interrupt this important line of questioning but we must have a word from our sponsor.

Mortenson: Sponsor?

Contd.

Lyons: (Using the pause to sneak forward for one last dirty blow) Medicare!

Thump: (Cracks whip, sings like ringmaster)

There's no reverence any more
For the people who mind the store
Now. . . back you vicious, you
fiery beasts
And let the sponsors say a word, at least.

(Chases reporters offstage)

Moderator: (Smiling uneasily) And now a word for our Sponsor, Jumbo Ju Ju Bits, the dog food candy that makes people jealous of their pets. . .

(Screams and howls and whip crackings from offstage.)

Moderator: (Keeping straight face, holding up a box of Jumbo Ju Jus) Jumbo Ju Jus keep your doggie smiling. . .

(Crash and snarling and the crack of the whip again offstage.)

Moderator: . . . because its got special K9-75 tooth brightener for dogs. And have you ever been bothered by doggie's bad breath? Well in new Jumbo Ju Jus, hexophosphate formula 43Z22TL-74W-19-J24Q with tetrahydrine keeps doggie's breath almost kissing sweet. And now back to our program. . . (Looks offstage, befuddled. No one comes.)

(Long pause)

Moderator: (Embarrassed) There's no one here. . . (Stalling) Only me. . . (Very nervous) I've never had to say anything all by myself. . . (Looks offstage for another long pause) . . . Well, we could talk a bit more

Contd.

Moderator: (Continuing) about Jumbo Ju Goo . . . (tongue tied) I mean Jungoo Boo Boo Jits. . . I mean. . .

(A whip cracks offstage. Moderator collapses into chair relieved. Snarls of "Taxes" "War" from offstage. One by one, the reporters come running onstage, look around frantically, and hide behind their chairs. Thump comes strutting in, holding whip and stool casually.)

Lyons: (Meekly peeping out from behind chair) Poverty!

Thump: (Cracks his whip, sings)

Say it again
A little more nicely
Say it again
A little more wisely

Lyons: (Singing) Poverteeee. . .

(Thump smiles.)

Mortenson: (Snarling) Corruption!

(Thump cracks whip twice. Mortenson whimpers.)

Mortenson: (Singing) Corruption. . .

(Thump points to both Lyons and Mortenson, cracks his whip, and they sing "Poverty" and "Corruption" in two-part harmony.)

Contrary: (Leaps from behind her chair snarling) Taxes! Freedom! Pollution!. . . (viciously going toward Thump.)

(Thump cracks whip again, holding stool in front of him, forcing Contrary up on her chair, where she hunches, clawing weakly.)

Lyons: (Sings again) Poverty. . .

(Thump cracks whip again at Lyons, chasing her from behind her chair. She takes position hunching like a lioness on the chair.)

Contd.

Mortenson: (Singing in last burst)
Taxes! Oh our taxes
We've got stacks and stacks of taxes. . .

(Thump cracks whip. Mortenson yipes and hunches up on top of his chair.)

Thump: (Singing to all)

And now we are ready
To push on ahead
To find ourselves a better world
By going where we're led
Now all of the people can have
Harmoneeeee. . .
And we'll reason together, you'll see.

(Thump cracks whip three times. On the third crack he motions to Lyons, who sings: "Poverty", to Mortenson, who sings low part: "Corruption" and to Contrary, a soprano: "War". And then to all three, who sing in unison: "And that's the American way, oh yes, And that's the American way. . . . ")

(Thump, hand on heart, turns and makes a long bow to audience. Sings:)

Well I couldn't have said it better
myself
When all is said and done
Government is fun
If all dissenting choices
Make a harmony of voices
Well then. . . I couldn't have said
it better myself. . . oh yeah
I couldn't have said it better myself.

(Another long bow and Lights Out.)

End

Floor Plan and Production Notes

The Beat the Press set is essentially a representation of several "face the issue" television programs. It could possibly be played in the round but would usually be laid out thusly:-

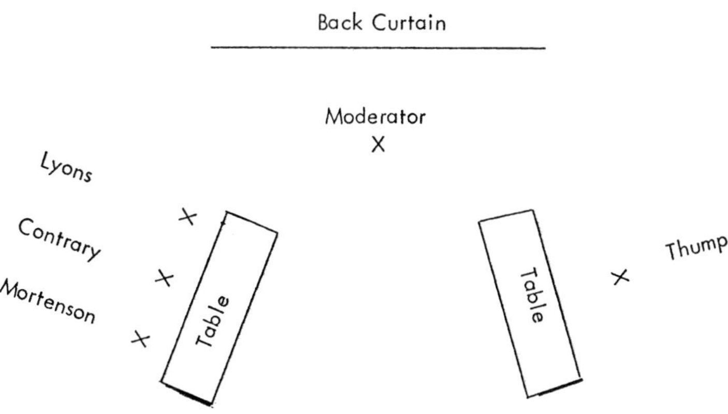

Senator Thump never says a word which is not in song. A more organic substitution than a whip might be a belt which he takes off for use in taming reporters.

The music to this play might be handled in several ways, but here is left out to stimulate creativity on the part of production people. One way might be to parody musical numbers, another would be to have original music written. And a third possibility, especially feasible if piano accompaniment is not available, is for the actor playing Senator Thump to sing whatever comes to his mind in the way of music. There are no restrictions for this is essentially a play and not an opera.

Visiting Hours

a one-act play by

David C. Hon

Cast of Characters

Tricia) Margo) Shirley) Darlene)	All very obviously pregnant, young unwed mothers-to-be
Andrew	A visiting father-to-be

Setting - The visiting room of an unwed mothers' home.

(VH)

(Four pregnant girls, Margo, Tricia, Shirley and Darlene sit in a semi-circle. Margo is reading a magazine, Tricia is knitting, Darlene is nervously twiddling her thumbs, and Shirley is playing with her swollen stomach as if a baby were in her lap, saying "goo-goo", playing peek-a-boo, and breaking into tears. The others, in their turns, leer over at Shirley's carrying on.)

Margo: (Looking up from her magazine) Shirley . . .

Shirley: (Back from her daze, looking up at Margo as if she has been caught) Oh . . . I'm sorry, Margo . . . I know you don't like me to do that.

Tricia: (Stopping her knitting) It's just . . . grotesque . . . That's what it is . . . grotesque. (Looks solemnly, as if her last word should kill.)

Shirley: (Hanging head) I'm sorry . . . I won't do it any more . . . (Brightens a little) It's just that I . . . The thought of my own . . . (Holds her stomach).

Tricia: Well, it's not your own . . .

Margo: It's going to be adopted out the minute you see it . . .

Tricia: You'll be lucky if you're awake to see them take it away.

Margo: (Coolly,decisively) You should hate it . . .

Shirley: (Hanging head again) I know . . . (Smiling slightly through tears) . . . I should . . . But somehow . . . (Looking down at her stomach again) . . . I don't.

Contd.

Tricia: You ought to hate it . . . It's taken a half-year of your young life . . . And you've been disgraced by it . . .

Margo: She's a fool . . .

Shirley: (In tears) I'm not a fool . . . I'm silly, but I'm not a fool . . . I love my baby.

Margo: (Scornfully) You have no baby to love . . . You signed the paper . . . It's the adoption agency's baby . . .

Shirley: (Bravely mounting a smile through tears) But right now . . . (Staunchily) . . . It's mine.

Tricia: Little fool . . .

Margo: We're all fools, Tricia . . . (Pointing to Shirley) she's just a double- fool . . . Plain fools learn . . . Double-fools fool themselves into thinking they aren't fools . . .

Shirley: Sometimes I think . . . (Turning to Margo) I could keep my baby, you know . . . I could live at home and work . . . A lot of girls do that . . .

Margo: (Disgruntled) Double-fool!

Tricia: (Mocking) You signed the paper . . . You declared that you would not be a fit mother and you accepted their board and room and doctors and . . . (Viciously) You are no better than the rest of us . . . We're stalks of corn,

Contd.

Tricia: (Continuing) sitting here ripening . . . We're . . . (Cackles morbidly) . . . For all of the rehabilitation crap . . . (Cackles again) We're on a *Baby Farm*!

Margo: Hey that's right! . . . (Playacting) How's it going, Farmer Tricia?

(Both Margo and Tricia rise and walk around like fat farmers.)

Margo: How's the *crop* this year?

Tricia: Oh, jes fine (pretends to pick her teeth) . . . Got me a good seed this time . . . Be pickin' pretty soon . . . Looks like a good yield, all in all. . . Hybrids, they are, a little a this and a little a that . . .

Margo: If you need a couple of hired hands come plantin'time, I got the numbers of a couple a boys in town . . . Oh, they ain't good for much, drinkin', runnin' around all the time . . . But when they work, they work hard . . . Worked hard for me last plantin' time . . .

Shirley: (Sobbing) Stop it! . . . Please . . . (Drying tears on forearm) . . . Please stop it . . . It was so easy signing those papers a few months ago . . . Before it started . . . *Being* . . . inside me . . .

Tricia: (Incredulously) Forget it, sister . . . The only way you're going to get that baby is to get someone to *marry* you . . .

Shirley: (Regretfully) I know . . .

Contd.

Margo: (Mocking again) And what are you going to do? . . . Advertise?

Tricia: (Cackling) What would you say . . . at 50 cents a line in the local newspaper?

Margo: (Musing) We bought lines for more than that . . .

Shirley: I don't know . . .

Tricia: You going to say: "Lovely Swollen Girl Needs Mate?"

(Tricia and Margo laugh)

Margo: Or maybe you'd be more *subtle* . . . You could put it in the investment section . . . "Young Man Needed as Partner in Small Corporation - Immediate Returns from Capital of Previous Investor," . . . (To Tricia) . . . Sounds good, eh? . . . Let's run it up the flagpole, eh, B. J. ?

(Margo nudges Tricia and they both cackle again.)

Shirley: (Shaking head) No . . . No . . . I know . . . You're right . . . I just want it . . . Already I love it . . .

Margo: (Scorning) Double-fool . . . Do you realize . . .

(Darlene, who has recently come out of her twiddling obscurity, now enters the conversation firmly.)

Darlene: Margo . . . You would make some man an excellent . . . *bitch*.

Contd.

Margo: (Surprised) Who asked you?

Tricia: Yeah, you were off there dreaming . . . twiddling . . . (Condescendingly) . . . waiting. . .

Darlene: (Defending) She's got her little foolish dream . . . She's just saying it for all of us, really . . .

Tricia: Not for me . . . I'm going to be a pill hound when I get out . . . No more babies for me . . . It's not my little dream . . . I'm going to buy a lifetime supply of pills and take three or four every day . . .

Margo: (Coming in strong) And it's not my (Pointing to stomach) little dream, either . . . Men are the reason . . . The whole reason . . . I say exterminate men and we'll have a better . . .

Tricia: (Thoughtfully interrupting) Well . . . not all men . . .

Margo: All men!

Shirley: (To Darlene) Thanks . . .

Tricia: (Pointing to Darlene) And you! . . . You are Miss Lilly White today . . . You and your (Mocking) male visitor . . .

Darlene: (Quietly) You've just no right to gang up on poor Shirley. . .

Margo: Right Schmeit! . . . We get enough crap here from Miss Burns . . . (Squints eyes) Suspiciously fat

Contd.

Margo: (Continuing) Miss Burns . . . (Rises and playacts, waddling around) . . . Scrub that floor! . . . (Points to one side) . . . *Scour* that toilet! (Points to *other* side) . . . Ha! . . . (Stops playacting) Miss Burns who's *fatter* than all of us put *together* . . .

Tricia: (In mock revelation) I'll bet . . . She's *pregnant* . . . Our overseer . . . *pregnant!*

(A chorus of lurid, scornful "Oooooh's" from all. They giggle together. Shirley continues giggling longer than the rest, and Margo stares at her.)

Margo: (Staring, speaking coolly now) As I was saying . . . We get plenty of crap without some double-fool foisting off tears . . . and dreams . . . and . . . (Utter mockery) . . . "*goo-goo's*".

Darlene: (Starting to defend), She's just . . .

Tricia: (Rudely) And what are you doing. . . sharing that little farce with her . . . You *waiting* there . . . For your *visitor* . . . All primped up . . . *What* makes you think he'll come? . . . (Squinting coyly) It's getting late now . . .

Darlene: It's a long drive from the city . . .

Tricia: (Shifting her attack now) Humph! A very long drive for a *father* . . . Too long . . . (Pauses, *and* breaks into a smirk) . . . He's not here and he's not going to be here . . . We're the *leper* colony, we are . . .

Contd.

Tricia: (Continuing) Little bells around our necks . . . We can't take a walk into this little town here (Motioning with arm) without those people giving that knowing nod to each other . . . (Gives a knowing nod to audience) . . . Little boys snickering, young men turning their heads away . . . (Pauses, then looks at Darlene incredulously) . . . What makes you think he'll come?

Darlene: (Calmly) He said he'd come . . .

Margo: He said he'd come before . . .

Tricia: (Stalking around Darlene) It's easy for your car to stall on such a long road from the city . . . You just turn off the key . . . (Mimes turning of key) . . . And . . . Surprise, surprise! . . . Your car just won't start unless you turn it around toward the city again . . .

Margo: (Also stalking around the seated Darlene) He lost his nerve . . . He can't look you in the eye . . . Any minute now you'll get a phone call saying he's lost his nerve and can't look you in the eye . . . That's what you're waiting for, isn't it? . . . That phone call, saying his car stalled again?

Tricia: (Playacting with imaginary phone) Hello . . . Hey sorry, my car stalled . . . See-you-later-bye . . . (Pretends to slam the phone down) . . . And slam! . . . (Holds on hips) That's all folks . . .

Contd.

Shirley: (Optimistically to Darlene) If he called that would still mean he cared some . . .

Margo: (Overhearing) You'll be lucky to get a phone call . . . If I lost *my* nerve a second time, *I* wouldn't even *call* . . .

Darlene: (Bravely) I trust him . . . He'll come.

Tricia: (Cackling) *Trust* him . . . She *trusts* him . . .

Shirley: (Consoling) I think he'll come, too.

Margo: It's going to be a lovely supper tonight, Tricia . . . Double-Fool and Twice-Jilted holding hands, filling their soup bowls with tears . . .

Tricia: Supper is only about an hour away . . . (To Darlene) He's not coming, Darlene . . . He's sitting there, getting ready for his own supper . . . (Inspiration) . . . Ah ha . . . It's Friday . . . Did you think of that? . . . Hey, imagine this if you can . . . (Digging) He's probably getting ready . . . Right this minute . . . To go out with some *hot date* . . .

Darlene: (Quaking. They have penetrated her armor) No!

Tricia: (Focusing her point) He's probably taking a shower, using scented soap . . . Probably has his cuff links and tie all laid out on the bed . . .

Contd.

Darlene: (Shaking head, trembling) No!

Tricia: Has the moodiest records all set out . . . The sexy blue light in the lamp . . . (Into Darlene's face) Clean sheets on the bed . . .

Darlene: (Contorting away) NO! . . .

Shirley: (Pushing Tricia back, forceful for the first time) Stoppit! . . . STOPPIT!

Darlene: (Relaxing back to gentle tremble) No . . .

(The telephone rings)

Margo: (Triumphantly) You'd better get it . . . *Darlene*.

(Phone rings again)

Shirley: I'll get it if you'd like, Darlene. . .

(Phone rings again. Everyone looks at the phone.)

Tricia: *Somebody* get it . . . I'd hate to have anyone think we're *not* here . . .

(Phone rings again. Margo rises to go for it.)

Darlene: (Rising, blocking Margo's way) No . . . (More composed now) . . . I'll get it . . . (Picks up phone) . . . Hello . . . Yes . . . This is Darlene . . .

Tricia: (Cackling) Ha! . . . He doesn't even remember her *voice*!

Contd.

Shirley: You shut up . . .

Darlene: (Turning her back and speaking more quietly) Yes . . . yes, that's fine. . . All right . . . Yes . . . I understand . . . Softly) Bye . . .

(Darlene hangs up the phone and turns, expressionless, to the others.)

Margo: (Mocking) Ha! . . . His car's stalled . . . Or what's his excuse this time?

Tricia: (I-told-you-so-ish) Anyway, he's not coming . . .

Darlene: (Sitting down, pausing lengthily) He's coming.

(Surprise on the faces of Tricia and Margo. Shirley jumps happily up and down in her seat.)

Shirley: I *knew* he would. We'll leave, Darlene . . . Right now . . . (Rises) It might scare him to see all of us . . .

Darlene: (Smiling happily) It will probably scare him to see *me* . . . (Looking at her stomach) *But* stay . . . Shirley . . . (Glares slightly at Margo and Tricia.)

Margo: (Rising to leave) Returning to the scene of the crime . . .

(Exit Margo)

Tricia: (Mocking) He'll probably stay two minutes and then *run* . . .

(Exit Tricia)

Cont d.

Darlene: (Explaining to Shirley) He got lost . . . He was always like that . . . Getting lost . . . Not on purpose, either . . . His mind was just on higher things . . .

Shirley: He must be very nice . . .

Darlene: (Moving her hand back and forth) Most of the time . . .

Shirley: Well, I'd better go . . .

Darlene: Stay until he comes . . .

Shirley: OK . . . (Musing) I *do* get a little silly over having a baby, I guess.

Darlene: (Unrelatedly) He wouldn't let me do away with it, you know . . .

Shirley: That's pretty strange . . . for a man.

Darlene: No . . . He said he was a big enough egotist to think that his child deserves to live more than most of the kids running around in this world . . .

Shirley: *You* wanted to, then . . .

Darlene: I did then . . . You know how everything runs through your mind . . . And some things seem so easy . . .

Shirley: (Nodding) Like getting myself in *here* . . . (Glances around) . . . Did you . . . (Prying) Did you ever talk about . . . Well. . .

Contd.

Darlene: (Shaking head) He didn't believe in young marriages . . . I mean eighteen is very young . . . (Thinks) . . . I guess he's nineteen by now . . .

Shirley: (Hapless) I'm only sixteen . . .

Darlene: Really?

Shirley: That's right . . . (Fishing) . . . Do I look older?

Darlene: (Patronizing) Sometimes . . . Sort of . . . (Changing subject) Anyway . . . That didn't look like a good way . . . So . . . Well . . . Here I am.

(Call from offstage - woman's voice - "Visitor . . . In your rooms. Close your doors.")

Shirley: That's him . . . I've got to go . . . (Rises) . . . But Darlene. . .

Darlene: Yes?

Shirley: Do you mind if I take a peek at him from my door as he goes up the hall?

Darlene: If you stay, I'll introduce you.

Shirley: No, no . . . (Excited) No, I just want a peek.

(Exit Shirley)

(Darlene is alone. She starts to rise, then decides to sit. She primps slightly. Footsteps are heard. She rises nervously and walks toward the door. Before she gets there, however, a young man puts his head in the door.)

Contd.

Andrew: Is this the . . . ?

Darlene: (Standing before him) Hello, Andrew . . .

Andrew: (Shyly entering) Hi . . .

(They stand nervously facing each other, hesitant to show emotion or affection of any kind.)

Darlene: (Finally) Well. . . Would you like to sit down?

Andrew: Uh . . . (Looking around) . . . Just anywhere?

Darlene: Just anywhere.

Andrew: (Fumbling) Well my coat . . . (Taking his coat off) . . . Could I put my coat on this chair?

Darlene: (As if out of daze) Oh yes . . . I'm sorry . . . Of course . . . (Takes his coat from him) . . . This is our visiting room, but I'm afraid we don't have many occasions to use it.

Andrew: (Biting lip) Uh . . . OK to sit here? (Motions to chair behind him.)

Darlene: Sure . . . Was it a bad drive?

Andrew: No . . . Not really . . . The snows melted off the highway . . . Just walking up here from the parking area . . . Got a little slushy.

Darlene: I'm really glad you came.

Andrew: Well I'm sorry about the other time. . .

Contd.

Andrew: (Continuing) My car stalling and all . . . I hope you didn't think . . . I'd . . . (Silence)

Darlene: (Breaking silence) No . . . I didn't think that.

Andrew: (Gazing at her) You're looking very pretty now . . .

Darlene: Oh . . . just . . . peaches and cream . . . (Looks at her stomach) . . . I wish you had been able to come a month ago, the first time . . . My . . . (hesitates) . . . It wasn't so big then.

Andrew: (Delicately musing) It's big *now* . . .

Darlene: It does things . . . Little dances on the ceiling and acrobatics . . . You can't imagine.

Andrew: (Nodding) I can't .

Darlene: Were you ever a gymnast . . . Or a dancer?

Andrew: No . . . I took a few turns on the basketball court before everyone outgrew me . . .

Darlene: (Nodding) Then that's what he's doing . . . He's dribbling my bladder like a basketball . . . There he goes again.

Andrew: It's a *he*, then?

Darlene: Not necessarily . . . I guess there are girl basketball players . . . So . . . (With an ever so slight crassness) What else is new, Andrew?

Contd.

Andrew: (Eyes go shifty) Well, I've been working pretty steady . . . And I got a high draft number . . . And with the money I've saved, I might be able to go to the University next year . . . (Gazes at her stomach again) . . . Say . . . Darlene. . . ?

Darlene: What?

Andrew: Say . . . Could I . . . I mean I'd really like . . . To touch it.

Darlene: You would? (Tears in eyes again)

Andrew: I mean . . . Don't cry . . . Please don't . . . I don't have to touch it . . . Just please don't cry. . .

Darlene: (Wipes her eyes, smiling) But, Andrew . . .

Andrew: (Ashamed) Forget I said anything . . .

Darlene: But you see . . .

Andrew: I'm sorry . . . Really . . . A plague on me for even thinking . . .

Darlene: (Taking his hand) But Andrew . . . I wanted you to touch it . . . But I couldn't ask, could I? . . . All along I wanted you to. . .

(Andrew lets her guide his hand to her stomach)

Andrew: (Pausing) Something's going on in there . . .

Darlene: It's a basketball game . . . If you

Contd.

Darlene: (Continuing) listen you can hear the cheerleaders - Pancreas, Appendix, Liver, Spleen - They're all there . . . (Pauses) Enjoying the game immensely . . .

Andrew: (Sympathetically) Are you?

Darlene: (Softly) No. . . not much.

Andrew: (Withdrawing his hand, pausing) I could have you out of here in five minutes.

Darlene: You mean . . . I thought we *decided* . . .

Andrew: (Pulling back) I didn't mean. . . No, I only meant . . . That we could go off together . . . Escape, sort of . . .

Darlene: But I'd have to come back. . .

Andrew: Well, we could escape for a while . . . Do you suppose they'd chase us?

Darlene: (Incredulous) Andrew . . . Who would care? People only chase people if they *care* . . . Who would care about a pregnant girl fleeing across the countryside? Who'd put up roadblocks?

Andrew: (Thinking) You could scream a little . . . Then it would be *kidnapping*.

Darlene: I don't *want* to be kidnapped.

Andrew: I guess it's pretty silly . . .

Contd.

Darlene: It's not silly . . . I just don't want to be kidnapped.

Andrew: No, it's silly. . . For me to be making wild statements . . . Just to . . . (Hesitates)

Darlene: You always made wild statements . . .

Andrew: (More slowly) Just to . . . (Hesitates again)

Darlene: And we did some wild things, too. . . (Not really talking to Andrew) . . . Remember the night we rode freight cars out to the farm town and then hitched back. . . And that drunk who picked us up ran his car into the garbage dump and we nearly froze getting back to the main road and it was all. . . (Smiling pleasantly in her reminiscence)

Andrew: (Awkwardly) I said it just to . . . cover . . . up. . . for. . .

Darlene: (Continues oblivious) It was all very beautiful with the garbage dump fires burning, reflecting in the river . . .

Andrew: To cover up . . . For the fact . . . That I still feel the same.

Darlene: (Pausing, as if coming back from a dream) Oh, Andrew . . . You blew it . . . Blew it right away. . . (Raging) Damn you Andrew! . . . It would have been so easy for me to have this child and let it go . . . If you just hadn't come . . . If you just hadn't said that. . .

Contd.

Andrew: (Apologetically) I just thought, being lonely here . . . That you might want to know.

Darlene: (Snapping) Well I *didn't* want to know. . . I wanted *to be* pregnant and jilted and let my damned flower of love die in its season . . . And go on . . . (Glaring) And you have to go and be the true, all-time *bastard!*

Andrew: Then do you still love me?

Darlene: (Shaking head) No . . . not at all.

Andrew: (Stricken almost, relaxes back in his chair) Not even a little?

Darlene: (Shaking head again) No . . . a *lot*.

Andrew: You're lying. . .

Darlene: No . . . I was lying before . . . But I don't want to marry you . . .

Andrew: But at least let's go . . . (Rises) . . . Let's get out of this . . . (Looks around) . . . *Institution*. . .

Darlene: Only. . . If you'll promise me you *won't* marry me . . .

Andrew: (Lying) Uh . . . I'll make my best effort . . .

Darlene: (Shouting, but in good humor) NOOOOO!. . . I want a promise . . . I won't go without a promise.

Andrew: (Shuffling) All right . . .

Contd.

Darlene: (Insisting) Not "All right" . . . say: "I won't marry you."

Andrew: (Hesitating, looking at the floor) I won't marry you . . . I promise.

Darlene: (Jumps up, elated) I'll just grab a bag on the way by my room . . . (Kisses Andrew) . . . Andrew . . . I love you. . . I really dearly do. . .

(Both Exit, running hand in hand)

Lights out

The End

Floor Plan and Production Notes

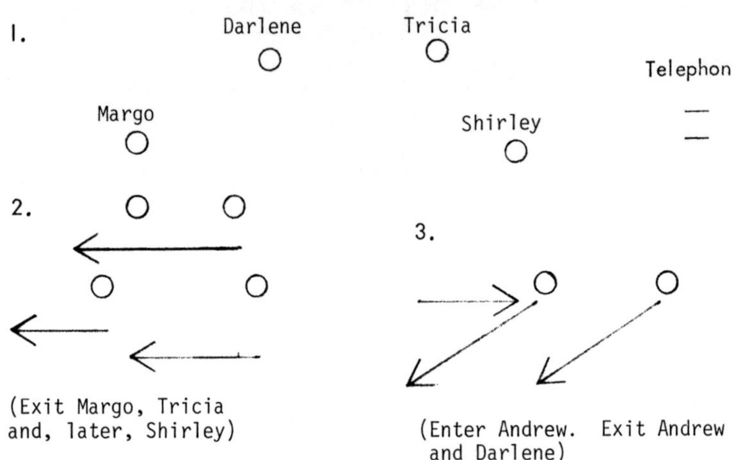

Visiting Hours is a light modern love story. It should be played comedy but some people may try to make it ponderous and profound.

The girls should definitely be in the bulging stages of pregnancy and should walk and move in this manner. As early in rehearsals as possible they should begin wearing their padding.

The telephone can be a poignant force, as telephones ringing on a quiet stage are. Care should be taken to pace dialogue to convey maddening hesitation between rings.

Gunfight

a one-act play by

David C. Hon

Cast of Characters

Wimple		
Sykes		
Alma	-	Wife of Wimple
Sarah	-	Girlfriend of Sykes
Orville	-	Town grocer
Slade	-	A gambler

Time is 1880. Place: Old West. The stage is blank.

(GF)

(Enter Wimple, holding a pistol)

Wimple: Where is Sykes? When I find him I'm going to put so much lead in him... (Shouts) Sykes, where are you?... Come out here and fight like a man.

Sykes: (From offstage) Put your gun away, Wimple, and I'll fight you man to man.

Wimple: (Putting gun in his holster) All right... But bring your gun... You've been saying sweet things to my wife... You were talking to her in the grocery store.

Sykes: (Still offstage) There's no harm in that, Wimple... I didn't mean anything...but I'm not afraid of you, either.

Wimple: We both know the real reason... and if you're not afraid, come out here.

Sykes: (Entering, his hand near his gun) You'll be eating dirt if you fight me, Wimple.

Voices: (From offstage) He's right, Wimple. He's the fastest man in Texas.

Wimple: I'm not afraid of you, Sykes.

Sykes: Then you must be drunk.

Wimple: I always drink whiskey for breakfast, but I'm not drunk. You're almost a dead man, Sykes.

Contd.

Sykes: Give me one good reason why . . .

Wimple: I've got two good reasons. If one doesn't work, the other will work. The first reason is: I'll be faster than you.

Sykes: I doubt that.

Wimple: The second reason is: I've got my friend Orville. He is standing behind you with a gun.

Sykes: That's an old trick, Wimple. (Confidently) I'm certainly not going to look.

Wimple: You don't have to look. You can feel his gun in your back.

(Orville comes behind Sykes and holds a gun in Sykes' back)

Sykes: (Looking sad) The second reason is a good one.

Wimple: (Smiling) Of course. Are you ready to fight now?

Sykes: Not yet.

Wimple: I thought that you were ready.

Sykes: First, I want you to know something. My girlfriend Sarah, has a gun in <u>your</u> back.

Wimple: (Laughing) That's a joke. I won't believe that.

Sarah: (Coming from behind with rifle) This gun will help you to believe.

Wimple: (Surprised) You were such a nice girl, Sarah.

Contd.

Sykes: You've got your friends and I've for mine.

Wimple: Unfortunately for you, my friend Slade the gambler is behind Sarah right now.

Sykes: He's the only man in town who will shoot a woman.

Slade: (Sinister) That's right.

Wimple: And in addition, my wife is behind you with another gun. Are you ready to fight now?

(The formation of people on the stage now is: Alma and Orville holding guns behind Sykes, and Sarah and Slade holding guns behind Wimple.)

Alma: (To Orville, quietly) After Sykes kills my husband, you and I can go away together.

Orville: (Nodding, turns to Sykes) Don't worry. . . Wimple's wife loves you and I have an argument with Wimple, too. We won't interfere.

Sykes: (From the corner of his mouth) Thank you, Orville. But I still have to decide about Slade.

Slade: (To Sarah) You and I can go to Dallas together. I want you to see some good times. (Touches her back with his free hand.)

Sarah: (To Slade) First we have to eliminate Sykes.

Slade: (To Sarah) That's no problem. Orville is going to shoot Sykes after Sykes shoots Wimple. Orville thinks he is going away with Alma.

Contd.

Sarah: In that case, Alma is going away with Orville?

Slade: No, she really loves Sykes. She will shoot Orville because he killed Sykes.

Sarah: I feel sorry for Wimple.

Slade: Don't feel sorry for Wimple. I owe him money.

Sykes: Are you ready, Wimple?

Wimple: I was ready when I came.

Sykes: There is one thing of importance, and you ought to know it. Your wife Alma and Orville are going to run away together after I kill you.

Wimple: What? , Alma, is that true?

Alma: No, it's not. I love Sykes.

Wimple: Why?

Alma: Because he says nice things to me in the grocery store.

Orville: (To Alma) Then you were deceiving me.

Wimple: Sarah, do you still love me?

Slade: What?

Sarah: No, I don't love you, Wimple. I love Orville. And after Orville shoots Sykes, Alma and Slade will go away together. (To Slade) Alma told me everything.

Sykes: Wait a minute...Alma is going away with Slade...and Sarah is going away with Orville.

Contd.

Wimple: (Confused) I just want to shoot somebody.

Sykes: But listen... I ought to shoot Orville and you ought to shoot Slade.

Orville: But I really love Alma. I said that to Sarah because I wanted Sykes to kill Wimple.

Slade: And I really love Sarah ... I told that to Alma because I wanted her to let Orville shoot Sykes.

Wimple: (More confused) I just want to shoot somebody.

Sykes: But listen...In that case, I ought to shoot Slade and you ought to shoot Orville.

Alma: Is that true, Slade? Do you really love Sarah?

Sarah: Is that true, Orville? Do you really love Alma?

Wimple: Why doesn't anybody love me?

Orville: Then Slade, you rat, you are going to take my Alma.

Slade: And you're going to take my Sarah.

Sykes: The answer is simple. Why don't you trade?

Alma: How can you trade me? I love Slade.

Sarah: Orville, you said so many sweet things to me. Now you don't love me.

Contd.

Wimple: I just want to shoot somebody. Maybe I'll shoot everybody.

Sykes: I have an idea, Wimple. Let's go get a drink.

Wimple: Without shooting anybody?

Sykes: Maybe they'll shoot each other.

Wimple: You're right. I ought to have a drink and think about the best person to shoot... You know something? You're not such a bad man, Sykes.

(Sykes and Wimple exit. The four remaining face each other, standing in a square pattern.)

Orville: Well...

Slade: Well...

Alma: Well...

Sarah: Well...

Slade: Maybe we ought to take a card. (Brings out several playing cards) The highest two get each other.

Sarah: Love doesn't happen that way.

Orville: I don't know how it happens.

Alma: Maybe I ought to return to my husband.

Slade: I knew it. Now you want security.

Sarah: And maybe I ought to return to Sykes...perhaps I have loved him all the time, Orville.

Contd.

Orville: (Turning to Alma) Alma, don't you know now? I've loved you all these years.

Alma: And I loved Slade ... (Looks at Slade, then shakes her head.)

Slade: (To Sarah) Sarah, don't you want the good times in Dallas?

Sarah: No, I like my bad times with Sykes.

(Sarah and Alma exit)

(Orville and Slade look at each other. Slade is laughing.)

Orville: You caused this, Slade. You pretended to love Alma, and then she pretended to love me. She wanted me to let Sykes kill her husband.

Slade: You caused it, Orville. You pretended to love Sarah. Sarah loved you but she pretended to love me. She wanted to protect you from Sykes.

Orville: What do you mean? You're responsible because you love Sarah.

Slade: No one is responsible when he is in love ... Or else you are responsible for loving Alma.

Orville: That was a different matter.

Slade: (Shaking head) No ... It was the same thing ... We lost ...

Orville: Sarah loved me ... But I didn't love her. If you don't have the right person to love, it is better to have *nobody*.

Contd.

Slade: Alma loved me ... If she comes back, I will take her. If you don't have the right person to love, it's better to have somebody.

Orville: That's immoral.

Slade: That's life.

Orville: (Becoming angry) It is not life ... Maybe it's your life. You play with people like cards, trying to find the high one.

Slade: (Sneering, laughing) That is life ... you idiots ... you dreamers ... Your type of man loses thousands of dollars to me ... Because you see either all or nothing ... The highest card or nothing ... The one you love, or nothing ... (Laughs cruelly) You are idiots, all of you ... I take percentages.

Orville: And your kind of people ... You ruin everything with your percentages ... You'll take anybody to love.

Slade: (Laughing) I'll take somebody ...

Orville: (Going toward his gun with his hand) You are the cause of it all ...

Slade: (Faster to his gun) You are the cause ... (Points it at Orville) I simply want somebody ... (Fires)

Orville: (Falling, holds out his gun) Nobody ... (Fires at Slade)

(Both men lie dead on the stage)

Contd.

(Enter Alma and Wimple hand in hand, followed by Sarah and Sykes, also hand in hand.)

Wimple: What happened?

Sykes: Someone heard them. They were talking about love.

(The two couples stand in a straight line behind the bodies. Wimple and Sarah, nearest to each other, bend over for a closer look. At the same time, Sykes makes a motion toward the side of the stage and holds up five fingers for Alma. Alma smiles and nods assent. Wimple and Sarah stand upright again and Sykes and Alma appear innocent.)

Wimple: Strange things happen.

Sarah: It's very romantic. They died for love.

(Alma and Sykes now bend over for a closer view. Sarah's hand reaches out bashfully for Wimple's. Wimple smiles bashfully. As Alma and Sykes stand upright again, Sarah and Wimple quickly pull their hands to their sides.)

Sykes: I wonder what they were arguing above?

Alma: We will never know.

Wimple: Well, we ought to be going.

Sykes: I suppose you are right.

Alma: Goodbye, Sarah.

Sarah: Goodbye, Alma.

(As the two couples leave the two sides of the stage, first Sykes and Alma look back across the stage, and nod and smile. Then Sarah and Wimple do the same.)

(All exit.)

Curtain

Floor Plan and Production Notes

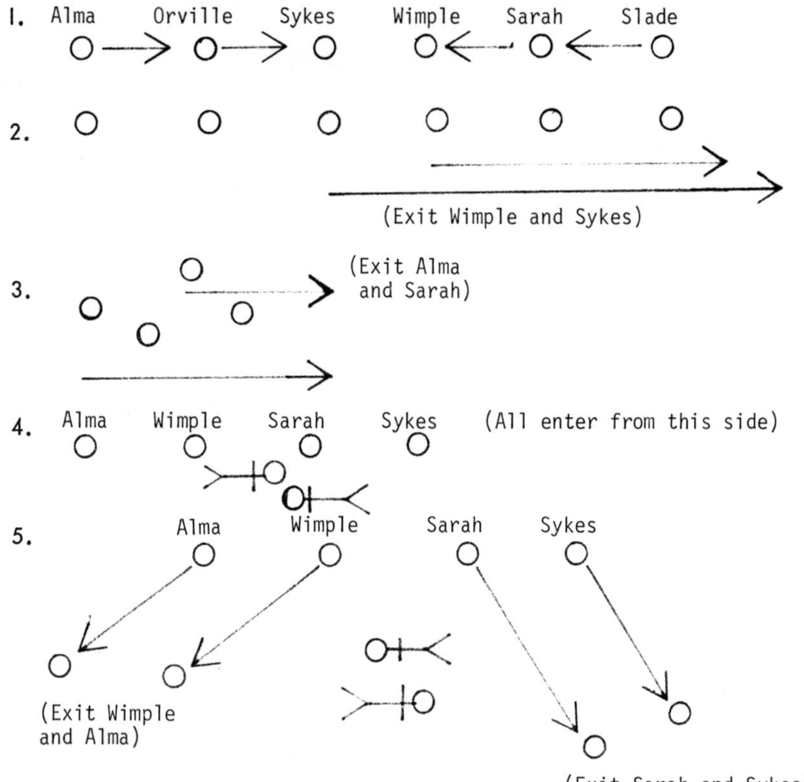

Gunfight is the mixture of many effects: confusion brinking on understanding, numerous eye-gags, well-paced reaction and stylized freezing while other lines are said. Quite crucial are the ending flirtations between Wimple and Sarah, and Alma and Sykes letting the audience continue in their mind the game which goes on and on.

Props include pistols and cowboy hats for Sykes, Wimple and Slade. A pistol and shopkeeper's apron for Orville and two rifles for Alma and Sarah.

The Mannequin

a one-act play by

David C. Hon

Cast of Characters

The Mannequin
Hank
Alfred
The Hag

(Lights on. The Mannequin is standing posed in a suit of the latest female fashion, exactly in the center of the stage. Alfred and Hank come in, dressed in work clothes. Alfred, holding a mop, looks around warily.)

Alfred: (Uneasily) I've never done this before.

Hank: Nothing to it. We just take the clothes off her and carry her away.

Alfred: But I mean this store window... It's like some kind of. . . of stage or something. . . (points out to audience). . . Do you realize all the people that walk down that avenue and look in this window? (Looks very nervous)

Hank: (Shaking head) Not at three o'clock in the morning.

Alfred: (Nervously looking back at the wings) I wish they'd left me in the shipping department. In shipping you can sleep sometimes, too.

Hank: (Assuringly) I've been doing this job for years now. Never seen more than a drunk or two with his nose up against the glass, tapping and hollering "take it off, take it off!"

Alfred: (Anxious) And did you?

Hank: It's my job. . .

Alfred: And what did they do. . . when you did?

Contd.

Hank: (Looking out to audience) They fogged up the glass a lot. . .

Alfred: I don't know if I'd have the nerve to do that. . . In fact I'm losing my nerve now. . . (Looks stage-struck at audience and backs toward wing). . . There's somebody out there. . . (Points) I tell you. . . There's somebody out there. . .

Hank: (Peering out at audience) I don't see anybody. . . Maybe there's some low life back in the shadows. . . (Pauses, turns to Alfred) You can't let it get to ya, Al.

Alfred: It's Alfred.

Hank: That's your first mistake.

Alfred: If I let everybody call me Al I'd be just another shipping clerk named Al.

Hank: I let you call me Hank.

Alfred: They introduced you as Hank.

Hank: Introduced?

Alfred: Yeah, they said "Hey Hank, here's the new guy".

Hank: You've got a good memory. That was five minutes ago.

Alfred: (Hiding behind mop and peeking out at audience) Hey Hank. . . Really. . . Doesn't it ever get to you, being out on a stage

Contd.

Alfred: (Continuing) here for all the drunks and cops and weirdoes?

Hank: Naw. . . not a bit. . . I even put on a little show sometimes. . . (Does a little tap dance). . . They love it. . .

Alfred: I could never put on a show. . . Hey, all we have to do is get this model undressed, right?

Hank: Then we've got the other windows.

Alfred: Yeah. . . But furnishings and kids' toys aren't so. . . You know. . . So personal. . . (He looks for the first time at the Mannequin. He is caught by something, and looks at her strangely for a moment). . . You ever feel personal about any of these?

Hank: (Stumblingly) Oh well. . . I know them. . . *apart*. . . If that's what you mean.

Alfred: You have names?

Hank: No, not names. . . But you can tell them apart. . . I mean this one here, this is a good one. . . Only chip she's got is behind her ear. . . (Shows behind ear)

Alfred: (Thinking a moment) Boy, I don't know how you could tap dance in front of people. . . (Struggles with little dance, cuts it off shyly.)

Contd.

Hank: I'll show ya some night kid. Maybe Saturday night when all the drunks come out.

Alfred: Oh, no. . . not me. . . (Revelation) But hey, you know I almost forgot about being out here.

Hank: No different than being anywhere else. . . No people out there now.

Alfred: Yeah. . . But there could be. . . I'd live in fear of starting to do something and looking back and having those eyes on me. . .

Hank: Whatever eyes are out there don't care (Looks out at audience). . . So we don't care neither, OK?

Alfred: But you've got to care.

Hank: Not me.

Alfred: But everybody sort of cares, about what they're doing and how they look doing it, I mean.

Hank: I care about my paycheck.

Alfred: (Gulping) Yeah. . . I guess I'll come to that. . . someday. . . (Changing subject). . . So you know all the girls, the models. . .

Hank: Sure do. . . Now this one is special. . . see. . . you can bend her arms at the elbow (Bends one of the Mannequin's arms upward) . . . The others they just have a solid arm and it looks funny here. . . (Demonstrates with his own arm) . . . Or here. . . (Bends his own arm backward).

Contd.

Alfred: Yeah, I see. . . (Bending the Mannequin's arm into different positions).

Hank: And her knees, too. . . See? (Pulls her leg up, bending it at the knee.)

Alfred: Yeah. . . Hey look. . . (Bends arms and legs into several different positions. Stands back to examine). . . Hey, yeah. . . This is a great one. . .

(Both men circle the Mannequin, looking for little things to play with.)

Hank: And her mouth even opens and closes (Works the mouth). . . And her eyes. . . Get this. . . (Pulls eyelids to half-closed). . . That's for when she's wearing high fashions. . . Makes her look kind of superior to everyone. . .

Alfred: This is a rather amazing model. . .

Hank: Expensive, she is. They only bought one of her kind. . . From some Italian clockmaker, I hear.

Alfred: Golly!

Hank: Well, we've got to get her in. . . Let's take off the coat.

Alfred: Here? Can't we just carry her inside?

Hank: Naw, all these expensive clothes slide around and get wrinkled. (Starts to unbutton suit coat).

Contd.

Alfred: (Looking over right shoulder toward audience) There's someone looking, Hank. . . I know there's someone out there looking.

Hank: (Sliding coat off to reveal white blouse) So they look. . .

Alfred: So I'm embarrassed. . . (Staunchly) But you're right. It's just a job. . . See? I've come to that already.

Hank: (Wearily) I hope so.

Alfred: (Examining her lower regions) She is well-built though. . . (Smoothes his hand down the outside of her thigh) And the ears. . . (Runs finger around inside of ear) . . . Except for the chip, it's a perfect ear.

Hank: (Folding the coat) Right.

(While Hank is turned slightly away, Alfred mischievously tiptoes up and blows in the Mannequin's ear. There is a minuscule sigh. Alfred jumps back, eyes wide open.)

Hank: What was that?

Alfred: (Looking strangely at Mannequin) Uh. . . That was me. . . I'm a little tired.

Hank: You only been here a few minutes . . . They must have worked too easy in shipping. . . (Pause, holding folded coat indecisively). . . Uh. . . Listen. . . I've got to get a box for these clothes. . . Can't lay them down for a second, cause the day manager gets mad if they're dirty . . .

Contd.

Hank: (Continuing) Just wait a minute and I'll find one. . . You be taking off the rest of the clothes.

Alfred: (Gulping) Me?

Hank: (Beginning to exit) Yeah *you*. . .

Alfred: But Hank. . . I mean you can't leave me to. . . (Hands out pleadingly)

(Hank exits shaking head)

Alfred: (Pacing hesitantly around model) Oh my God.

(Resigning himself to duty, Alfred starts to pull a shoe off, then stops, rises slowly and looks Mannequin in the face.)

Alfred: Look. . . I really don't want to do this. . . (Sets Mannequin's foot down shoeless, rises again holding the shoe). . . I mean you're almost. . . almost *real*. . . (Looking into her eyes) Why your eyes are. . . intelligent. . . There is sadness in them. . . Or maybe callous determination. . . (Walking around her) But you are beautiful. . . (Thinking, pacing away for a moment). . . If only you could. . . (Idea) Listen. . . Do you think. . . Well. . . (Hesitantly). . . Well, no one has loved me for a long time. . . And it's not my fault. . . It's everybody else's. . . I mean I've got a lot to love. . . I'm kind. . . and gentle. . . But I'm strong in my own way. . . You have to get to know me. . . (Looks into her eyes again) Or maybe *you* don't. . . Maybe this is just one of those times when two souls meet, just run

Contd.

Alfred: (Continuing) together happily. . . Like little brooks into a river. . . (Pause) Do you think?. . . (Excited). . . Do you think that you could. . . love me?. . . (Holds her shoulders). . . I'm going to kiss you. . .

(An Old Haggard Woman staggers onto front of stage right, guzzling from a whiskey bottle. She stops and stares at Alfred kissing the Mannequin.)

Alfred: Those are wonderful lips. . . There is something very real about you. . . More real than most girls.

(Hag looks incredulcusly toward audience.)

Alfred: Do you suppose. . . If I helped a little bit. . . You could say that you love me?. . . I'll move your mouth. . . And say the words. . . But the feeling will come from you . . . (Moves her jaw slowly) I. . . Love. . . You. . . (He fawns backward) She loves me. . . Well, you wouldn't have said it if you didn't mean it, would you?

(Hank shouts from offstage: "Hey, you got those clothes off yet? I gotta go downstairs for a box".)

Alfred: (Panicking) Yeah, okay. . . (To Mannequin) I can't do that. . . I promise you I'll defend you. . . My little lotus blossom. . . (Beams) . . . Now see, an ordinary girl would have laughed at me for saying that. . . But I've always wanted to say it. . . To someone. . . (Repeats sacredly) My little lotus blossom. . . And you love me, so you understand. . . Everything. . . (Moves to kiss again. Just as lips touch, Hag in background cackles loudly.)

Contd.

(Alfred whips around)

Alfred: (Peering out) Who's that?

Hag: (Still cackling) I'm her fairy godmother. . .

Alfred: (Seeing that she holds a whiskey bottle, moves closer to front of stage, shouting) You go away!

Hag: (Mocking) It's a free street. . . Go on. . . I was just enjoying the show. . . I'll bet she's never been kissed. . .

(Alfred is enraged but is trapped inside)

Alfred: Get out of here. . . (Presses fingers to imaginary glass.)

Hag: If you put on a good show, I'll turn her into a real live girl. . .

Alfred: Away! Go away!

Hag: (Pressing her fingertips to his on her side of the imaginary glass) You don't want a real live girl? . . . (Backs off, drunkenly cackles) They never do. . .

Alfred: (Still pressing his fingertips to the glass) Why won't you go away? What do you want?

Hag: (Momentarily pushing her hands to his again) Do you really want to know?. . . (Turns away, speaking softly). . . I want someone to care for me, like you care for that doll girl. . . If there were a chance of that. . .

Cont

Alfred: I can't hear you!

Hag: (Still softly) I want. . .

Alfred: I *still* can't hear you!

Hag: (Whipping about, shouting) I want a *show*!

Alfred: (Backing away, as if stricken) Oh, well I couldn't. . .

Hag: (Puts hands up to window) I *deserve* a show. . .

Alfred: (Panicking) I just work here. . . I just. . . (glancing at Mannequin, then grabbing mop). . . I just mop up. . .

Hag: (Pointing at Mannequin) You put on a show for her.

Alfred: (Gripping mop) That's different. . . That's none of your business. . .

Hag: It is my business. . . I'm more real than she is. . . (wiggles hips). . . any night.

Alfred: (Confused, looks at Mannequin) She's right. . . I think. . . Is she right? You can open my soul, but that live woman. . . I detest her. . .

Hag: I can't hear you. . . When do I get my show?

Alfred: (Thinking) If I do a show will you go away?

Hag: Try and see.

Alfred: (Struggling to begin a tap dance) How's that?

Contd.

Hag: Terrible. . . (Cackling). . . That's so bad I'm leaving.

Alfred: No. . . stay. . . I can do better . . . (Taps furiously across the stage)

Hag: Sorry. . . I've got better things to do .

Alfred: (Still dancing furiously) The best part is coming. . .

Hag: (With desultory wave) See ya. . . (Staggers offstage).

Alfred: (Stops, breathing heavily) Well. . . (To Mannequin) You see how it is . . . I didn't even care about her. . . And when I started caring. . . She got bored. . . You understand, don't you?. . . Don't you? (Alfred nods her head with his hands). .. I thought you would. . . (Listens) . . . Hank will be back in a minute . . . Oh God. . . And then I'll have to take your clothes off. . . Listen. . . I couldn't undress you . . . in front of. . . (Looks over shoulder out to audience). .. them. . . (Grabs around Mannequin's waist and pulls her toward rear wings).

Hank: (Appearing from left rear wing) Here's the box. . . (Sees Mannequin) What the hell?. . . You were supposed to get her clothes off.

Alfred: (Blubbering) Well I. . . There was this drunk lady, see. . . and. . .

Hank: (Grumpily) Well we haven't got all night. . . (Starts to take off hose, shoes).

Contd

Alfred: (Stepping dramatically out in front of Mannequin) No.

Hank: What?

Alfred: (Holding mop viciously) You lay a hand on her and I'll. . .

Hank: But we're running late. . . I mean what the hell?

Alfred: (Ferociously) You lay another hand on her and you'll get this between the eyes.

Hank: Try over the top of the head.

Alfred: (Undaunted) Whatever. . . (brandishes mop).

Hank: Look. . . OK. . . I'll take her in the back and do it. . . You just stay out here and mop. . .

Alfred: (Pouting, relaxing) OK. . . (Pointing finger) But you don't bring her back here without clothes on, see?

Hank: (Grabbing Mannequin) OK. . . OK.

Alfred: Not without clothes, do you hear?

Hank: (Not quite frightened, but cautious) Yeah, OK, just put that thing down.

(Exit Hank with Mannequin)

(Alfred, alone on stage, doesn't know which way to turn. He looks longingly toward the rear of the stage, back of which his "love" is being "raped").

(Hag staggers back into front of stage. Looks strangely at him and then to audience.)

Contd.

Hag: (Puzzled) I must have gone around the block. . . (With finger). . . Right, and then right. . . and then right. . . and then. . . Right. . . I thought I made a left back there somewhere. . . Maybe that was yesterday. . . (To Alfred) Hey. . . Hey, you.

Alfred: (Preoccupied with rear of stage, finally reacting to Hag) Yes?

Hag: Where's your friend?

Alfred: In there. . . she's. . being changed.

Hag: (Drunkenly) Aw, why don't you put on a show?

Alfred: Don't feel like a show. . . (Sulking)

Hag: (Mocking) Oh. . . Did they take her away from you?

Alfred: No, I just let her go. . . I just stood here saying Okay. . .

Hag: Well then. . . What's all the. . .

Alfred: (Hands against glass) Listen you old hag. . . Do you know what it's like for me. . . It's as if she's in there being *raped*. . . .

Hag: Raped?

Alfred: (Sadly) Yes. . . raped.

Hag: (Surprised) Oh. . . (Fishing in deep coat pocket) Oh well in that case. . . (Pulls out a sleazy old wand, and smiles) . . . She might as well *enjoy* it.

Alfred: What do you mean?

Contd

Hag: Is she back there?

Alfred: Yes, but. . .

(Hag takes swig from bottle in her left hand and makes quick tiny circles in the air with the wand in her right hand.)

Hag: This takes concentration. . .
(Swigs again)

(Alfred stands back perplexed. Hag reacts to the slug of whiskey, circles the wand a few more times, and points it to the rear of the stage. A long scream echoes from the rear.)

(Alfred is transfixed, paralyzed. Moments later Hank comes out scratching his head.)

Hank: The damndest thing, Alfred. . .
I just can't. . . It was the
damndest thing. . .

Alfred: (In a wave of joy) Then she was. . .
(Glances to Hag) Don't change
anything. . . You sweet lady. . .
(Runs off stage, shouting) Hey, hey
where are you? Do you remember
a few minutes ago, what you said?
Do you remember, I kissed you?

(Alfred is gone, running after his love. Hank looks strangely at the Hag, as if he can't quite make her image out through the vagueness of years.)

Hank: Is it. . . ?

Hag: Hello, Hank.

Hank: That girl. . . You did it again. . .
Like you did when I was young. . .
and you were younger. . .

Hag: I've been around. . . Took to the
bottle. . .

Hank: It's been a long time. . .

Contd.

Hag: (Musing meditatively) Yeah, I did it again. . . (To Hank) It's why you stayed in window dressing, isn't it?

Hank: Yeah. . . I guess so. . . Always looking for the right one. .. Another one who would come alive for me. . . Just for me. . . That first one left me, you know. . .

Hag: I know.

Hank: Said I treated her like a mannequin . . . How do you treat her like a woman when she still wants to be a mannequin?. . . Dressing fancy. . . Holding poses. . . Always aloof and superior. . . How do you treat her like a woman?

Hag: (Pauses, then kindly) Hank. . . Do your show. . . It was a nice show. . .

Hank: (Looking back to rear wings) And now he's got it to go through. . . (Sadly) Jesus, I don't envy him. . .

Hag: Smile, Hank. . . and do your show . . . I'll clap. (Begins clapping)

Hank: Ah yes. . . OK. . . (Begins to soft shoe). . . Ah. . . Takes me back. . . (Smiles) Takes me back along the years. . .

(Lights as he soft shoes off stage)

End

Floor Plan and Production Notes

The Mannequin cannot be played in the round because the impression to be attained is that of a display window in a large city department store.

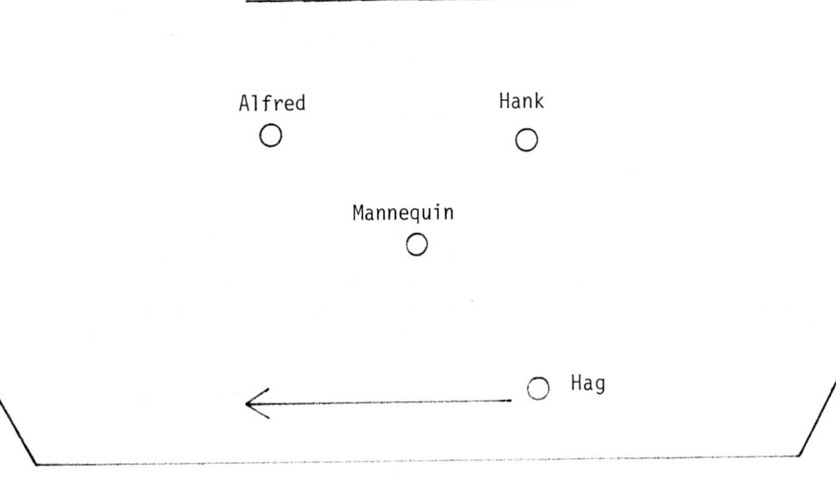

Three things are absolutely essential to this play:-

1. That the Mannequin never move of her own reaction or volition.

2. That all dialogue directly between the Hag and either of the two workmen be shouted, as if through glass.

3. That once the window has been established by any movement of any player, that window must be maintained <u>exactly</u> by all other players.

One timing element is especially important. When the Hag points her wand to the back curtain, the scream must issue as if as a direct result of that wand being pointed.

The First Atheist Church

a one-act play by

David C. Hon

Cast - The Minister

Setting - One pulpit, facing audience.

(FA)

(Lights On to the empty pulpit standing in front of audience. For several seconds they will be allowed to wonder about and identify the pulpit. The Minister then appears, in full-length dark robe, and takes a standing position behind the pulpit.)

Minister: Good morning. . . Before we start our services this morning, I would like to say a few words about our fantastic growth. In only three weeks now, our congregation has nearly tripled in size and, in these days, when churches are failing left and right, I think that represents a great public response to our message. . . I'd like you to know also that our building fund and blood drive are both going very well, and I am especially proud of our Sunday School. . . You know, teaching our children to be good atheists is a *big* part of making a better world for all men and. . . (Smiles) By golly those youngsters are just eating it up. . . When I see their bright little faces as they take their little red color crayons and underline contradictions in the Bible, well. . . I just *know* we're right. . . So now let us go into our first joyous song, which is on page 43 of your New Atheist Hymnal:

(Organ music, taped chorus, mimeographed songs - any of these may be used as supplement as the Minister steps from behind the pulpit to lead his "congregation" in song, swinging his arm, coaxing the song out of them.)

Minister: (Leading the song to familiar tune)

Onward Atheist soldiers, now we shall be heard
Shouting through eternity, our Almighty
    Word.
Fighting back temptations to believe in God,
Forward into nothingness though people
    call us odd.

Contd.

(Refrain)

Onward Atheist soldiers, now we shall be heard
Shouting through eternity, our Almighty Word.

Onward Atheist soldiers, marching in the fore,
Calling all religion, all a needless bore.
Faith we call insanity, Hope is ne'er to be,
Charity is self-seeking and Love, hypocrisy.

(Repeat refrain.)
(Minister finishes song with benign look over congregation.)

Minister: (Beaming) A truly beautiful song. . . one to give us strength when we are persecuted, to glory in when we feel that glow of life that no one gave us, that is just there. . . (Opens his text) And now, a responsive reading from page 121 of your Manual for Atheists or, as the second entry on your program of services. As you know, you answer to each thing I say with the response: "So it was, and so it is, and so it ever shall be."

(Steps out from behind pulpit again to coax more participation from the congregation. Until they follow, the Minister may have to say the words to the response, drawing them out of the mouths of the audience.)

Minister: (Beginning) From nothingness we came and to nothingness we go, and why, asks the Visitor, need we ask for more?

Congregation: (Hopefully) So it was, and so it is, and so it ever shall be.

Minister: And if eternity be foreboding, what comfort can we give to all aho face it? We say. . .

Congregation: So it was, and so it is, and so it ever shall be.

Contd.

Minister: And to the child, beckoning
for some eternal answer, we say
of life - "Enjoy".
For:

Congregation: So it was, and so it is, and
so it ever shall be.

Minister: And to the lost and low in
spirit, we offer this consolation:

Congregation: So it was, and so it is, and
so it ever shall be.

Minister: And to the prosperous man, happy
in his home, his children bright
and healthy, his wife a trusting
partner . . . What can we say
to him?

Congregation: So it was, and so it is, and so
it ever shall be.

Minister: And at the age of wisdom, when
all mysteries but death seem
insignificant, how can we comfort
these old ones? By saying,

Congregation: So it was, and so it is, and
so it ever shall be.

Minister: And lastly, when our being seeks
itself to its utter depths, when we
wish to shift our troubles on to
some convenient diety, and when
we resist, looking earthward, we
smile and say . . .

Congregation: So it was, and so it is, and
so it ever shall be.

(Minister smiles benignly, and moves again to his place behind the pulpit.)

Contd.

Minister: Before we turn to our next song, and pass the collection plate, I want to remind all the ladies of the sewing circle next Tuesday night at Melba Powers' house . . . These ladies are doing a great thing, making blankets for the outcast victims of the world's holy wars . . . That's a lot of blankets, I know . . . But that's our ladies for you, always in there helping out the poor and needy . . . And when the holy wars are over, we have another project, to help out Christians who are bankrupt after their Christmas spending . . . (Reflective) . . . Yes . . . There is a place for good Atheists in this world . . . (Proceeding) Now let's go on to our next song . . . On page 82 of your New Atheist Hymnal, or the second song on your program . . . This one has a fine little melody and, even if you're not a singer, just join in on the chorus . . .

(Steps out from behind the pulpit again to lead, using same procedure as with "Onward Atheist Soldiers".)

Minister: (Singing)

Faith of our fathers led us to this,
It is a faith, which none of us miss.
When skies are dark, the world forlorn,
We feel our triumph when we can scorn.

(Chorus)

Faith of our fathers, lost in the past,
We will despise thee to the last.

(During this last chorus, the Minister takes a collection plate from the pulpit and starts it through the audience.)

Contd.

Minister: (Continuing singing the second verse)

When wars and fa--mine lead us to woe,
There is one thing that we all know:
God didn't do it to purge us of sin;
We claim it all as the failings of men.

(Chorus)

Faith of our Fathers, lost in the past,
We will despise thee to the last.

(The collection plate returns, undoubtedly empty, and as the song ends the Minister looks at the empty plate pathetically.)

Minister: Well . . . (Looking up at audience) That's one thing about we Atheists . . . We never make a big show of giving . . .

(Minister moves back behind pulpit, putting collection plate away.)

Minister: (Smiling as he launches into sermon) You know, there are a lot of things people admire about we Atheists and . . . (Holding up one finger) . . . I believe that is why our congregation is growing every week . . . Just the other day I had a man ask a member of our congregation why he was an Atheist, and I think the way he answered could be instructive to us all. He said: "I'm an Atheist because it really doesn't matter to me where we all started." And the questioner said "Well, then, you're an <u>agnostic</u>, not an Atheist." . . . And our member answered him . . . And I think we should all be proud of that answer, he answered: "No . . . I'm an Atheist. An agnostic would say 'I don't care' but

Contd.

Minister: (Continuing) but an Atheist will say 'It doesn't matter'" . . . (Pauses to let this sink in) "It doesn't matter." . . . Do you see how . . . how cosmic that answer is? The agnostic cares only for himself and what he thinks, but the Atheist . . . my brethren . . . The Atheist cares equally for the whole universe in that he doesn't care at all. . . .

(Minister smiles benevolently and lets this last sink in.)

Minister: That gives you a warm feeling right here . . . (Holds his heart) . . . Doesn't it? . . . A wild feeling . . . a free, daring feeling, doesn't it? . . . To know that there is no evil . . . For instance . . . Off the top of my head, if a man were to ask me "Isn't anything evil?", I would say, "Of course not." And he might say "Well, what if a man carried your little daughter away?" . . . (Pauses) . . . I'd say "Well, the man must have had deeply-felt psychological needs . . ." . . . Do you see? Nothing is evil . . .

(Pauses to look out over audience.)

Minister: But my brethren, we have the heaviest burden of all, and that is to rationalize everything we would ordinarily call evil. . . . We must take every foul act which comes into our day, and show that it is not really evil . . . That it is the product of society's forces, that it comes from repressed needs, or that it may benefit someone in the long run . . . We

Contd.

Minister: (Continuing) . . . We, my brethren, must shoulder this burden for the world in which most men shift their burdens to God . . . As if God were some kind of spiritual donkey . . . And in doing this, my brethren, in showing such a logical mercy to the guilt-ridden world . . . (In measured tones) We will become gods . . .

(Smiles and relaxes slightly, watching this sink in to audience.)

Minister: Now that's a pleasant thought isn't it . . . But when you stop and think about it, if man was meant to be anything, he was meant to be a god . . . So God came from earth . . . Isn't that a nice concept? . . . God, the son of man . . . (Holding finger up) . . . But you must remember your task, for the only evil in the world is the naming of good and evil, and the only good in the world is the God-like refusal to sit in judgment . . . Now that sounds like a paradox, I know . . . For who in the world should sit in judgment but those of us who see everything so clearly, we who see the evil of naming good and evil ... And the goodness of bearing uncertainty, of making uncertainty liveable. . . . It is our day-to-day martyrdom, my brethren, but in the end it will be worth it . . . We are the chosen people, chosen to become gods by calling the universe good . . . (Reflective) . . . Did you ever think how close are the words God and good? . . . (Thinks for a moment) . . . But then I didn't mean God is good . . .

Contd.

Minister: (Continuing) . . . I didn't say that . . . What I meant was that when we become God-like we will see everything as goodness, in that the Universe basically has no evil and all that has been created is good . . .

(Pauses long and meditatively, shuffling through mental notes. He is beginning to be in metaphysical trouble.)

Minister: (Quizzical) Somehow I think that has been said before . . .

(The flash of a terrible thought shows in his eyes, arrests his speech. He gulps.)

Minister: Well, let me re-state that, going back to the idea of our freedom because nothing really matters . . . (Hopefully) . . . Remember? . . . This is a great sense of freedom we have, my brethren, knowing that there is no evil . . . Even though it is a burden at the same time . . . This is because we always know we are free to choose between the evil of calling things evil, and the good of calling things good . . . (More confidently) The choice is ours . . . We are free men, we Atheists . . . Free to choose between good and evil . . .

(The terrible thought shows in his eyes again.)

Minister: That doesn't sound right, does it? . . . (Glimmer of hope in eyes) Ah yes . . . If we choose the good we become gods, but if we choose evil we become the slaves of it, vicious and calling things evil. . .

(The Minister is caught in his own web of contradiction, and his eyes flash panic.)

Contd.

Minister: (Frustrated) That doesn't sound right either. . . Well . . . Let me summarize if I can, and then it will all become clear to you. . . I hope. . . If we deny the existence of evil we will become gods, you see. . . men who have found the Universe to be good and who are free of those chains of evil. . . Happy. . . Oh yes. . . Happy in the worship of what is, because what is, is good. . .

(Pauses, thinks, winces, gulps)

Minister: But then. . . (Reasons looking from one pointed index finger to the other). . . I would matter that the world is good. . . (Frantic) . . . And it would follow that. . . (Gulps). . . And it would follow that. . .

(Turns away for a very long moment, then comes back.)

Minister: (Looking very lost) This is all very embarrassing. . . I mean it would follow that. . . (Moves hand to mouth). . . Oh God. . .

(His eyes are wild now, and his jaw hangs open, as he looks around like a man totally revealed, and drops to his knees by the altar, looking up.)

Minister: (In sheer terror) Oh. . . my. . . God. . .

Lights Black

End

(FA)

Floor Plan and Production Notes

The pulpit placement is obvious, with as short a distance to the audience as possible. This is because the Minister will have to establish a rapport with the audience which allows him to lead them in songs and responsive reading.

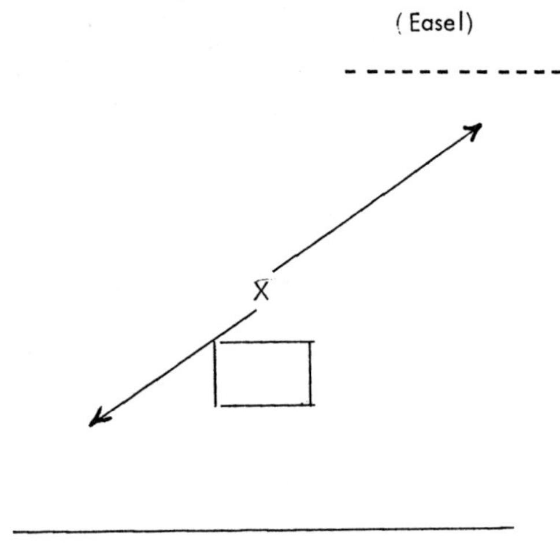

"Plants" in the audience help a great deal to stimulate this type of group participation and the use of an easel for the words of the two song parodies gives the audience all they need to join in. The return of the collection plate may also be an opportunity for a distinct reaction on the part of the Minister.

The Minister's metaphysical conversion must start when he says how similar are the words "God and Good". Where the production has been comic to that time, the progression of more and more uneasiness on the part of the Minister must begin early or the conversion will seem too sudden and lose the overall comic effect.

Murder Mystery

a one-act play by

David C. Hon

Cast of Characters

Inspector Thwart
Detective Pry
Dr. Fred Suture
Mrs. Breakwind
Mrs. Belcher
Miss Belcher
Miss Diddle
Dead Man

(The stage is black. It must be *utter* black. Lights go on. Six people sit in a semi-circle, open toward audience. In the middle of the open area lies a corpse, a man with a knife in his chest. The players seem as startled as the audience is when the lights flick on. Pause for the setting to tell its own story, and the play is begun by a blood-curdling scream from Mrs. Breakwind.)

Inspector Thwart: (Rising and leaning over to look carefully at the corpse. He bends over from the waist, hands on hips) . . . I believe . . . (He turns to Detective Pry) . . . Detective Pry, I believe there has been a murder here . . . Right before our eyes.

(Mrs. Belcher now screams long and loud, outdoing Mrs. Breakwind.)

Detective Pry: Well . . . Not really before our *eyes* . . . I mean the lights were *out* . . .

Inspector Thwart: Quite so . . . And Doctor Suture, could you give us any hints to this case?

(The Doctor goes into immediate action, feeling, opening eyelids, doing Doctor things. Finally he shakes his head.)

Detective Pry: Well?

Inspector: Well?

Dr. Suture: He's dead.

(Miss Diddle lets forth the most bloodcurdling scream of the evening. The assemblage looks at her curiously as she stands exhausted after the scream.)

Thwart: (After long pause) Miss Diddle . . . (To all) . . . Ladies . . . Whatever happened to . . . *fainting*?

Pry: (Back at the corpse) Well . . .

Contd.

Pry: (Continuing) It's fresh . . . We know that. . . I mean just moment ago, he was here among us . . . Talking and joking . . .

Mrs. Breakwind: Tapping his fingers . . .

Mrs. Belcher: Scratching his behind. . .

Miss Diddle: Picking his nose . . .

Dr. Suture: We all hated him. . .

Thwart: Then someone in this room must be guilty. . .

Belcher: But I had just arrived. . .

Pry: He was alive when you arrived. . .

Belcher: Well, yes. . .

Thwart: (Defending) But then so did we all. . . we all hated him and we all arrived before the lights went out and he. . . (Throws his hands up). . . Died.

Breakwind: He hated all of us, too. . .

Dr. Suture: And we all hate each other.

Thwart: Well, it is a murder. . . so it is a case for the police. . . (Gesturing to himself and Pry, who beams and nods). . . So I guess I'd better start somewhere. . . Now I have a theory. . . I want the person who hated this man most to raise his hand. . .

(Looks of astonishment on all faces)

Thwart: That's right. . . voluntarily now. . . I want the person who hated this man most to raise his hand. . .

Contd.

(All hands go up)

Thwart: (Surprised) Well. . . So much for *that* theory. . . You see the theory was that the guilty person would think that I would think that the guilty party would never raise his hand. . . (Thinks). . . Or something like that. . .

Miss Diddle: (Interrupting) But *I* know who the guilty party *is*. . .

Thwart: (Interested) Oh. . . That could make this case much easier. . . Who?

Diddle: (Hesitantly, looking warily around) It is. . .

(Lights suddenly black. Moments of black silence.)

Voice of Breakwind: Who turned out the lights?

Voice of Detective: It must have been the killer.

Voice of Dr. Suture: (Quietly) Miss Diddle. . . I wanted to tell you I find you quite attractive.

Voice of Diddle: (Breathless) Oh, really. . . Oh that's nice. . . But I don't think you should do *that* right now, Dr. Suture.

Voice of Suture: Do what?

Voice of Diddle: (Sighing) Oooooh. . . Do what you're doing with your *hand*. . .

Contd.

Voice of
Suture: (Surprised) But. . . I'm not doing *anything* with my hand. . .

Voice of
Pry: (Officious) It's my hand. . . I'm just looking for the light. . .

Voice of
Breakwind: Yoo hoo. . . Detective Pry. . . I think the light is over here. . .

Voice of
Pry: Where?

Voice of
Breakwind: (Fluttering senilely) Over he--re. . .

Voice of
Pry: Am I getting closer?

Voice of
Breakwind: Yes you ah---re. . .

(A crash of chairs and bodies is heard.)

Voice of
Pry: I fell over the body. . .

Voice of
Breakwind: It could have been such a lovely evening. . .

Voice of
Belcher: The light is really closer to *me*. . .

Voice of
Pry: I'm coming, Mrs. Belcher. . . Am I getting nearer?

Voice of
Belcher: Yes, you ah-re. . .

Contd.

Voice of Diddle: (Enjoying) Um. . . Dr. Suture. . .

Voice of Suture: My dear Miss Diddle, it may be forever before that light goes on. . .

Voice of Diddle: (Sighing) And that's so nice. . . Doctors have such nice hands. . .

Voice of Suture: But. . . I'm still not touching you. . .

Voice of Diddle: (After a little squeak) Is that you again, Detective Pry?

Voice of Pry: No. . . I'm over here now. . .

Voice of Diddle: If it's not you, Doctor, and not you, Detective Pry. . . Then it must be. . .

Voice of Pry: Closer now, Mrs. Belcher?

Voice of Belcher: Oh yes. . . I can feel your hot breath. . .

Voice of Diddle: Then it must be. . . The Inspector!

Voice of Belcher: Detective Pry?

Voice of Pry: I'm coming. . .

(Another large crash is heard)

Contd.

Voice of Pry: (Groans) I just fell over a second corpse. . .

Voice of Diddle: Inspector Thwart! You are a nasty man!

(Lights on suddenly. . . All eyes are immediately on Inspector Thwart, who lies dead with a knife in his chest.)

Miss Diddle: (To the dead Inspector). . . Oh. . . I'm sorry.

Dr. Suture: (Running to corpse, looking him over, looking back up) He's dead.

(Mrs. Breakwind bellows forth another bloodcurdling scream.)

Detective Pry: (Heartfelt) My Inspector. . . I shall take over your case and . . . (Standing staunchly up, holding his heart) . . . See it to its bitter end.

(Mrs. Belcher blasts forth a bloodcurdling scream, totally out of any context. All eyes turn toward her a bit jaded.)

Dr. Suture: (Disgusted) Really now, Mrs. Belcher. . . Timing. . . Timing . . . The effect was not right because your scream was not at all well-timed.

Detective Pry: That's not the problem here. . .

Mrs. Breakwind: There's more than one problem here. . .

Detective Pry: The problem is: Who's doing all this killing?. . . Now I have a theory. . . Which I have never

Contd.

Detective Pry: (Continuing) used because my superior, Inspector Thwart, always had his theories. . . But now, as you see, Inspector Thwart is dead. . . (Beams). . . And it is time to try *my* theory.

Miss Diddle: (Waving hand) But *I* know who did it!

Detective Pry: (Ignoring) Now in this theory. . .

Dr. Suture: (Pointing to Miss Diddle) She *knows* who did it. . .

Detective Pry: (Ranting, jumping up and down) *My* theory. . . 20 years on the police force and this is the first time I can try my theory. . .

Miss Diddle: But. . .

Detective Pry: (Pointing at Miss Diddle) *People* can be wrong. . . But a good theory, a correct verifiable theory. . . Can never be wrong. . . Now my theory. . . Goes something like this. . .

(Lights suddenly out. From the dark silence issues the most bloodcurdling scream of the evening.)

Voice of Suture: That was much better timing, Mrs. Belcher, much better. . . (Lecherously). . . And now, Miss Diddle.

Voice of Belcher: I didn't do *that* scream, Doctor.

Voice of Pry: Who touched me? Who touched me?

Contd.

Voice of Suture: I'm only touching Miss Diddle. . .

Voice of Diddle: I wish you would. . . I'm over here. . .

Voice of Suture: Excuse me, Detective Pry.

Voice of Pry: That's all right. . . Really I'm looking for Mrs. Belcher.

Voice of Belcher: For me? Me. . . oh dear. . . oh how lovely. . .

Voice of Pry: I mean I'm looking for the light. . . I have now stepped over the two bodies and I will be at your side in one moment. . .

Voice of Belcher: (Singing) I'm wai--ting.

Voice of Pry: (Singing flat) I'm coming. . .

(A crash is heard)

Voice of Belcher: Oh, Detective Pry, you don't have to kiss my feet. . .

(Lights suddenly on. Detective Pry is pulling himself up from the floor and looks back to what he fell over. It is Mrs. Breakwind, with a knife in her chest. Mrs. Belcher starts to scream, and Detective Pry clamps his hand over her mouth.)

Detective Pry: (Weightily) Mrs. Belcher, it is past the time for screaming.

Contd.

Dr. Suture: But what about your theory?

Detective Pry: Unfortunately, my theory included Mrs. Breakwind who, as you see, is no longer with us.

Miss Diddle: But *I* know the *answer*. . .

Detective Pry: I've been meaning to ask you about that. . . But we must do something about these lights first. . . (Looks to Dr. Suture)

Dr. Suture: I know nothing of lights. . . Of *bodies* (Looks longingly at Miss Diddle) I know something. . . But lights. . .

Mrs. Belcher: (Pointing to first corpse) He knew something about lights. . . He was an electrician. . . He. . .

Miss Diddle: How did you know that?

Mrs. Belcher: He was my husband by a previous marriage.

Detective Pry: All of which is totally beside the point. . . Now. . . Miss Diddle. . .

Miss Diddle: Yes?

Detective Pry: Who did it?

Miss Diddle: (In the limelight) You didn't think what I said was very important *before*. . .

Dr. Suture: *I* did. . . (Proud of himself)

Miss Diddle: Well, I'll tell *you* then. . . (Moves to whisper to Dr. Suture)

Contd.

Detective Pry: (Stopping her) I can't have this. . . You will have to tell all of us.

Miss Diddle: Why should I?

Detective Pry: The rules say so.

Miss Diddle: Oh, all right. . . It was. . . You know, if you had only thought a minute, you would know. . .

Detective Pry: (Tapping foot insistantly) Who was it, Miss Diddle?

Miss Diddle: It was. . .

(Lights black again)

Voice of Diddle: *Doctor Suture*. . . You don't *waste* any time, do you?

Voice of Belcher: Ah ha. . . Dr. Suture. . . It was Dr. Suture then.

Voice of Diddle: No it was not Doctor Suture. . . I just said that because of. . . Well. . . His *hands*, you know. . .

Voice of Belcher: Well who *was* it then?

Voice of Diddle: It was. . . Are you listening, Detective Pry?. . . Detective Pry?

(Lights on. . . Detective Pry lies dead on the floor, beside the three other corpses. Mrs. Belcher has her mouth open to scream when she sees him, but can't force one out. Miss Diddle and Dr. Suture break apart as if discovered by the light.)

Miss Diddle: (To Suture) Now don't you feel bad?. . . While we were doing. . . That. . .Detective Pry was being killed.

Dr. Suture: (Grimacing, setting jaw) And now it falls to me. . .(Eloquently) To pick up the torch, to carry on this investigation.

Mrs. Belcher: (Holier-than-thou, pointing) You might begin by investigating the murder instead of Miss Diddle.

Miss Diddle: Some people think I'm worth investigating. . . (Catty) You would like to be investigated too, wouldn't you, Mrs. Belcher?

Mrs. Belcher: Well. . .

Miss Diddle: (Forcefully) Wouldn't you?

Mrs. Belcher: Well. . .

Miss Diddle: Of course you would. . . All women love to be investigated.

Dr. Suture: Mrs. Belcher will be investigated too.

Mrs. Belcher: (Gratefully) Oh, thank you. . . Thank you. . .

Dr. Suture: But first I must ask Miss Diddle. . . Who killed these people?. . .

(Lights black. . . There is a blood-curdling scream.)

Voice of Suture: Oh my God. . . Have you been killed, Miss Diddle?

Contd.

Voice of Diddle: No. . . I'm fine.

Voice of Suture: Then it was. . . (Pauses) . . And the murderer is. . . (Pauses, clears throat). . . It is no wonder that you know who did it, Miss Diddle. . . And although I am deeply in love with you. . . I consider it my duty to. . .

Voice of Diddle: But I didn't <u>do</u> it.

Voice of Suture: (Confused) Oh. . . (Pause) . . . Are you certain?

Voice of Diddle: My love for you is as strong as your love for me, and on that love, I swear it.

Voice of Suture: Ah then. . . We shall have to live with this mystery. . . Meanwhile, we can resolve a few things in darkness. . . Where are you?

Voice of Diddle: Right here. . . Come to my arms, Dr. Suture... Quickly!

Voice of Suture: Ah yes. . . and now my love. . . Ah, how I love the touch of you . . . How I have longed to do this. . .

Voice of Diddle: You are caressing either Mrs. Belcher or Mrs. Breakwind, both of whom are now dead.

Contd.

Voice of Suture: (Gasping) Oh. . . I'm sorry. . . Where are you, Miss Diddle?

Voice of Diddle: Over here. . . That's right. . . (Passionately) Oh, Doctor Suture. . .

Voice of Suture: (Lecherously) Oh, Miss Diddle. . .

Voice of Diddle: (More passionately) Oh, Doctor Suture. . .

Voice of Suture: Call me Fred.

Voice of Diddle: (Highly passionate) Oh, Fred. . . Now. . . Now. . . Before we die. . .

(Lights on. . . Suture and Miss Diddle are caught in an embrace, and break apart quickly)

Dr. Suture: (To Miss Diddle) Before we. . . Die?

Miss Diddle: Yes, there is no time to lose. . . (Throws her arms around Suture) It's now. . . or never.

Dr. Suture: But. . . Right out here in the light?

Miss Diddle: It doesn't matter. . . Nothing matters. . . Have some sweet life with me. . . We'll both be dead soon. . .

Dr. Suture: But who will kill us?

Contd.

Miss Diddle: Oh please please. . . One moment of joy before we die. . . While we still can. . .

Dr. Suture: (Taking off his coat) All right. . . All my dignity to the wind. . . (eyeing her). . . It's for a worthy cause. . . (Thinks) But . . . Who is going to kill us?

Miss Diddle: A vicious force, lurking in the shadows of Man's world. . . The same one who turns the lights on and off. . . Always. . .

Dr. Suture: (Excited and impatient) Who? For God's sake. . . Who?

Miss Diddle: The playwright. . . He's going to kill us. . . and we will be no more. . .

Dr. Suture: The playwright. . . My God, yes. . . (Frantic, looking around) We are only figments. . . Figments! My God how humiliating!. . . Quick, Miss Diddle. . . (Throws his arms out to her.)

Miss Diddle: I am yours. . . (Throws arms out to Dr. Suture.)

(Lights black. . . Sighs from Suture and Miss Diddle. Ten seconds of silence with lights black.)

(Lights on. . . All the characters lie dead on the stage. . . Miss Diddle and Dr. Suture in each other's arms. . . The other bodies strewn around, giving the impression of reckless, wanton slaughter. Lights stay on for ten seconds.)

(Lights Out)

The End

Floor Plan and Production Notes

Murder Mystery may be presented on any type of stage (in round simply by closing the circle of six chairs).

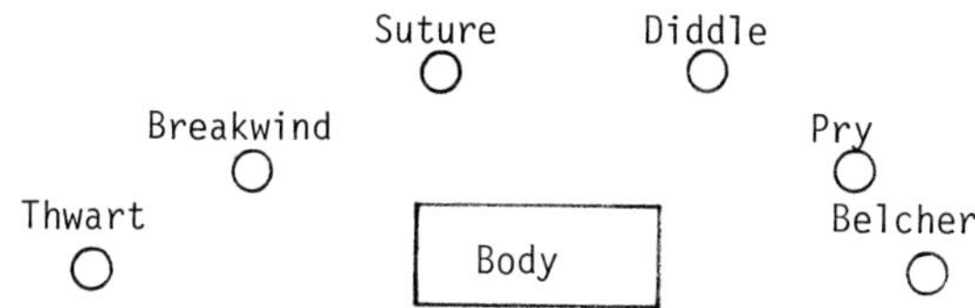

An aid to the success of Murder Mystery will be to get the darkest possible stage when the lights go out. For the possibility of some entering light however, simple movements should be blocked for the dark stage.

The danger of slow pace is intensified in Murder Mystery for some reason, and should be caught in early stages by the director.

While in the dark, the knife should be passed to the new body as soon as possible after the lights have blinked out.

A chaotic-looking body arrangement in the middle of the stage is most desirable. In order of their demise:-

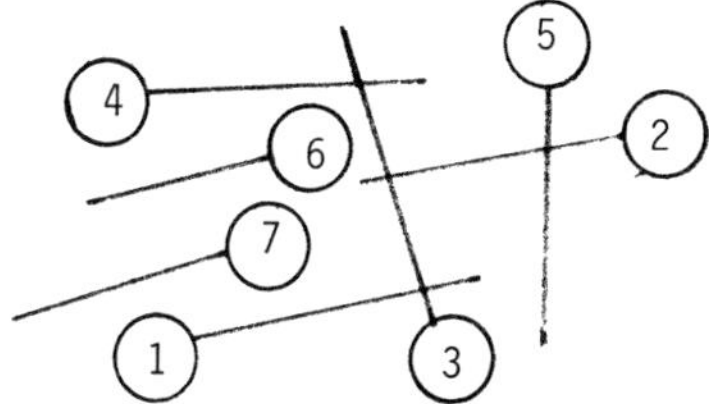

1. Already dead man
2. Inspector Thwart
3. Mrs. Breakwind
4. Detective Pry
5. Mrs. Belcher
6. Dr. Suture
7. Miss Diddle.

(This looks insane with real people. The trick is to pile them like firewood but to avoid crushing weight on anyone. Also be careful of stepping on fellow players in the dark.)

DIRECTOR'S NOTES

DIRECTOR'S NOTES

DIRECTOR'S NOTES

DIRECTOR'S NOTES

DIRECTOR'S NOTES

DIRECTOR'S NOTES

DIRECTOR'S NOTES